MEMOIRS OF A LYRICAL MAN

TAPESTRY OF TIME
BOOK 1

STEVEN TEMPLAR

MYSTERIOUS INK PUBLISHING

Memoirs of a Lyrical Man

The Tapestry of Time

Published by Mysterious Ink Publishing

Copyright © 2023 by Steven Templar

For Amy, who reignited the art

PROLOGUE

They call me Hagaki.

But I've gone by many names. A few you may have heard in passing at some point, but for the sake of avoiding confusion, I'll just refer to myself as Hagaki starting now. I've led an interesting life throughout the years. Or a few different ones depending on how you look at it. I know enough to blow a conspiracy theorist's mind a few times over. I can say this because it happened. He's not doing too well these days, poor guy. In the end, it was too much for him to comprehend. In my defense, it was hard having no one to talk to about my experiences, and he was more than willing to listen. I still take the blame for it.

I suppose the difference in writing my story instead is that you can digest it all piece by piece and have the option of putting the book down. Plus, it isn't being thrust upon you in a face-to-face setting by a rambling madman. And, of course, I'll label this as fiction so that you can easily pass it off as another fantastical sci-fi novel.

To say I've experienced a lot is an understatement. Three platinum records, a Grammy and an Academy Award. Okay, I never received an Academy Award, but I was nominated. It was a courtesy since I was friends with a few members of the committee. The movie itself was horrible. A movie about a rapper's life, *starring the rapper himself.* Who could take that seriously? It received decent reviews, but it was just a big advertisement for my latest and final album. And by final, I meant it. The pressure of being in the spotlight caught up to me fast. I was living the life I thought I always wanted, but I lost my friends and a part of myself. I've been alone before, but this was different. Being alone in the spotlight is a whole other monster. And I found a way out. That's why you've never heard my name before, even with all my accolades. Don't worry, I'll get to that.

Before I was a Polish-born rapper-actor, I was born in the town of Saitama, Japan. It'll all make sense soon, I swear.

1

————

I woke to lukewarm rainwater dripping over my face. The light rain tapped on the wooden roof, the weakest points conveniently over where I slept. My bed was surprisingly comfortable, considering it was just a pile of hay atop loose wood planks. I wiped the water from my eyes and rose, still sitting on the bed. My eyes were still adjusting to the dawn light creeping in through the windows as I realized my surroundings.

The room was small, but it had everything one would need to survive. On the opposite side of the room was a makeshift kitchen, complete with a large pot and crude utensils. Next to it was a small table with two chairs and a handcrafted lute resting in the corner. I felt at home, even though I wasn't sure where I was at first.

The confusion faded, turning into what I imagine it feels to have your head squeezed in a vice. The bigger details filled in first. I was around 20 or 30 years old, Japanese, a soldier of some kind. The dots in my head were being connected, the gaps beginning to fill in.

I rose from the bed slowly, slightly off balance. Using the wall as support, I regained my footing and headed towards the kitchen area. The pot had a small fire burning underneath it. In the water, a broth of vegetables simmered. Upon further inspection, I noticed the table was set for two. I tried to remember the past few days, but nothing came to me. My mind was a fresh notebook, with the details slowly being scribbled in.

I stopped for a moment and closed my eyes, trying to think as hard as I could about where I was. As I waited, the imaginary paper in my head filled with the details I was searching for. I was in a small village in eastern China. The memories sped up, flooding into my head making me dizzy again. I looked for something to brace myself against but only caught air. Almost landing on the table, I crashed down hard on the dirt floor next to it.

"Are you alright?" the voice screamed.

Dazed, I opened my eyes. Looking up from the floor, I saw a beautiful young woman drop her basket as she looked in from the doorway. Lijuan. The Governor's daughter. She wore an elegant dark green silk robe that draped close to the floor. The gold trim highlighted her dark shoulder length hair, giving it a warm glow. I remembered her father was in charge of the surrounding provinces of the village I had been calling my home. And I had asked for her hand in marriage not long ago.

I kneaded my fingers into my eyes, trying to get my focus back. "I - I don't know what happened." Through my blurred vision, I saw a haze of green and gold rush towards me.

"I told you not to stay in this shack overnight! You

might have caught something. Let me see your forehead." She put her palm to my head, which generated a concerned look in her eyes.

"You're burning up. Here, sit down and have some soup. I left it cooking for you while you slept."

"I'm sorry. I must have eaten something bad last night." The lie came instinctively, as if I was trying to protect my pride.

"No, I'm sure you have a cold. This drafty cabin is no good in weather like this, Hagaki."

Hagaki. Of course, my name is Hagaki! Despite all the recent memories flooding back, I hadn't even realized I didn't know my name.

Lijuan filled a bowl of soup and set it in front of me. "You really need to stop staying here. Just because some of the locals are giving you a hard time does not mean you have anything to prove. I love you and my father is quite fond of you, too."

I winced in pain as my vision blurred for a few seconds. Like a flash of lightning, yesterday came back to me. Last night I was visiting the local tavern for a late night drink. As soon as I walked through the door, I felt eyes on me. I'd been living in the village for a few months now, but ever since I announced my engagement to the Governor's daughter, a select few of the locals were completely against the union. By now I figured most of the naysayers had opened up to me, but tonight I was walking right into the lion's den.

I sat down alone by the bar and ordered a drink. The bartender was pleasant, or at least acted so, which I appreciated. The air was humid and I could feel the atmosphere changing since I had sat down. Dim lantern light flickered in the already dark bar, making it hard to see some of the surrounding faces. Most of the patrons eventually went back to their business, except for the whispering in the back corner. Halfway through my drink, they grew louder with more anger in their voices. I heard my name a few times throughout the conversation, which should have been my cue to leave. *Should have been.*

A firm hand gripped my shoulder. "You're not wanted here," the gruff voice rasped from behind me.

I set my glass down and turned to face him, still seated which broke his hold on me. I looked up to see Chaoxiang, the closest thing the village had to a bully. He was harmless most of the time, but he enjoyed causing trouble, especially when he drank. He stood over me with a glassy look in his eyes, clearly intoxicated.

I took a deep breath, searching for the most calming tone I could muster. "I'm just enjoying a drink, friend."

"We don't want you here. None of us do, outsider." He motioned toward a table, faintly visible in the darkness.

I focused in the direction and saw two other villagers eyeing me. One of them was cleaning his fingernails with a large knife. The other took a drink from his mug, keeping his eyes fixed on me the whole time. As he set the drink down, I noticed the table was littered with empty glasses. They were obviously drunk and were ready for a fight.

"You call me an outsider?" I shot back. I've had my run ins over the years, but something about tonight hit me differently. "I've lived in this land for well over a decade and you still call me an outsider? I left Japan over twenty years ago. They murdered my mother and brother before my eyes. I escaped with my life. I ask you respectfully, reconsider your opinion of me, friend."

He stood there with his eyes fixed on me. I got the impression that he hadn't expected that, considering when I first settled in the village, I had my own share of late night fights. After meeting Lijuan, I toned down my anger immensely and fought in a more diplomatic way. Oh, but I so wanted to kick his ass, believe me.

"You - you may have lived here long, but that gives you *no* right to marry my Lijuan," he barked back. "She deserves to be with a real man, not some scum born overseas!"

I rose from my bar stool and met his gaze. We were evenly matched height-wise, but he had a good forty pounds on me.

I stared at him with a neutral expression on my face. My lips curved into a faint smile. "I was just on my way out." I dropped a coin on the bar and headed towards the door.

The entire way out I overheard Chaoxiang calling at me, trying to goad me into coming back. I blocked his voice out of my head and walked out into the cool night air. The moon was almost full and illuminated the small lake surrounding the village.

I took a deep breath—proud of myself for being the better man and rising above instead of lashing back at him. I turned around towards the tavern just in time to see a fist flying straight at my head. I leapt to the side and grabbed the arm, twisting it behind my attacker's back in one smooth motion. Chaoxiang screamed in pain as I pushed even harder into his twisted arm. I felt something pop in his shoulder and immediately let go after realizing what I had done. It happened so fast that I didn't take into account that I had likely broken his arm.

He screamed again as he fought to stay upright, thrown off balance from the pain. "You'll pay for this, outsider!" Grasping his arm, he hobbled away muttering obscenities quietly to himself.

I could hear the patrons' chatter from the tavern—most likely trying to find out what had just happened. I picked up my pace and kept walking until I reached Lijuan's estate.

Lijuan lived with her father in an elegant mansion on the edge of the village. It was easily one of the oldest buildings in the area and no expense was spared in its decoration. Large arches stood in front of the courtyard, welcoming me into the gated perimeter. There was a small pond in the middle of the brick covered grounds, surrounded by red and yellow flowers. Trees with blue bulbs were scattered throughout, adding to the serene feeling I had whenever walking by. In the past I had come here to read or nap under the trees, but as of late I started to keep my distance.

Before the past few weeks, I had been staying in her father's guest house on the adjoining courtyard. It didn't feel right staying there, considering I wasn't officially part of the family yet. I didn't want to give villagers like Chaoxiang any more reason to spite me.

I turned away from the courtyard and headed towards the small cabin I had rented when I first arrived in the village. It was in bad condition, but it was all I could afford at the time, and it kept me warmer than sleeping outside.

The hike up to my cabin was always rough due to the incline of the hill and its distance from the village. To make matters worse, I was already tired from my sparring session with Yun, one of the royal guard. I finally reached the top of the hill and collapsed onto my bed.

2

———

"Hagaki, are you listening to me? My father hasn't been feeling well and he wanted us to come visit him today." Lijuan repeated, with a slight annoyance in her voice. I realized I had been deep in thought over yesterday and apologized.

"Damn right you're sorry! I heard you broke Chaoxiang's arm last night too! No doubt he deserved it, but did you really have to be so aggressive?"

"I tried to walk away, I truly did. I was just defending myself, I swear." I wished she was there to see how hard I tried to avoid fighting, this time.

"You're lucky he's one of the most hated men in the village, but it still doesn't look good for my future husband to be breaking arms and getting involved. Just try to stay away from the bar for a while, please love?"

I nodded apologetically. "I will."

"And you should really start staying at the guest house again. The hike up here is too much for me and it's probably making you sick staying on this old bed!" A giggle escaped her lips.

"I will, I will! For you Lijuan, anything." I rolled my eyes and flashed a mocking smile.

"Oh Hagaki, quiet you! Finish eating and get dressed so we can visit my father. He's expecting us soon."

WE WALKED in to find Governor Guo resting near a crackling fireplace. His room was adorned with elegant tapestries, from hand painted artwork to rich purple linens draped over the windows. He rose off his silk lined chair to greet us with a warm smile.

"Ah, I was expecting you! Please sit down." He motioned to the chair next to his near the fire. He embraced his daughter with a quick hug and whispered something in her ear. She nodded and exited towards the garden area of the courtyard. I sat down in the chair beside him and let my gaze drift to the fire.

"You know, I've always been quite fond of you, Hagaki." He paused and clasped his hands together, looking back with a solemn expression. "It was just over three seasons ago you saved my life from those barbarians, and for that, you have my eternal gratitude." We both sat in silence, focused on the fire. My mind drifted again, memories unlocking to fill the gaps in my head.

It was a cold night in the village. The first snowfall of the season had just begun. I was out looking for wood to keep the small fire in my room going when I heard a soft but curious thud. The noise came from the direction of the Governor's mansion. My curiosity piqued, I headed towards the noise to see three shadows headed straight for the mansion's front door.

The rest of the village was quiet and still, most likely bundled up in their homes to keep warm for the night. I crept closer to the courtyard, the smell of iron stronger with each step. And then I saw him. Broken and lifeless, one of the Governor's guards lay bloodied, thrown into the bushes.

In the distance, one of the shadows appeared to be wrenching at the door while the other two stood back and watched, weapons drawn. I was outnumbered, possibly alone, and weaponless, but the urge to help far outweighed my fear. The fallen guard's dagger bounced lightly in my tunic pocket as I raced around the other side of the mansion, still managing to keep my distance from the attackers.

Now on the opposite side of the intruders, I scaled the ivy covered lattice running up the side of the mansion wall. Nearly slipping from the cold sweat and ice on my hands, I made it to the second story and tumbled onto a balcony overlooking the courtyard. The window opened easily, allowing access directly to the Governor's room.

He lay peacefully, unaware of the oncoming threat. I crept closer, my hands pointed to the sky, hoping to rouse him without looking like an enemy. Soon realizing his shock either way, I shook him gently, whispering to get his attention.

"Governor, you're under attack. One of the guards is dead! You need to get up!"

He stirred for a moment before shooting upwards in

bed. Maybe it was his grogginess or he recognized me, he nodded then compiled and stood.

"The barbarians must be back," the Governor said in a raspy tone. "I have weapons in the cabinet over there." He motioned behind me. "Make sure Lijuan is safe."

The pounding of loud footsteps echoed outside the room. I scanned the room and pointed to the large curtains covering the balcony. "Hide behind those, I'll find her."

I grabbed the sharpest sword from the cabinet and started out the door. All three attackers were facing the other direction, looking into each room but gradually making their way closer down the hall. I hoped they hadn't found Lijuan and hid behind a large statue until the third passed by. The rest was hazy. Flashes of blood stained walls, screams, and eerie silence followed.

We both looked up from the fire at the same time. The knowing glance told me we were lost in the same memory. "I didn't call you here to talk about what happened last night. While I realize you come from a history of battle, your life is your own. However, as you soon wed my daughter, you must always strive for a more diplomatic resolution for the sake of my family name. Regardless, you know you have already received my blessing." He paused and cleared his throat. "But getting to the reason I called you here. We have more pressing matters on the horizon, and I need to be completely honest with you. The rumors you may have heard are all true. Recently, the Emperor sent an emissary to converse with me on the state of our nation."

"But they are known to check in on the provinces every now and again?"

"They are pushing their unification of our provinces harder than before. In the coming season, we will see more of a direct presence from the Emperor's Army." He took a deep breath. "They will station themselves inside the village and will start construction on a new statue in the Emperor's honor."

I heard the rustle of his clothing as he turned to face me, his gaze heavy with emotion. I could tell by his tone and expression that he had already made peace with the fact that he was powerless.

"This is all good news looking forward. Putting the people first is essential." I got the impression he was trying to persuade himself.

I hesitated to be direct, but I couldn't ignore the inconsistency I noticed. "Your downcast expression says otherwise."

"I feel as if my role here is coming to an end. The Emperor has the power to appoint any of his council to the province at will. If reports from the other areas are true, my time in power is limited."

"And what if you say no to him? To keep things as they are?"

"Ah young lad, the Emperor is wise, but ruthless. To do that would be spitting in his face. He would lay our village to ash at just the thought of going against his bidding."

"Is there nothing we can do?" I stood from my chair and slowly paced the room.

"I invited you here because I wanted you to hear this

from me directly. And to ask you to be my liaison to the Emperor's men when they arrive." He stood and began walking towards me.

I bowed slightly towards him. "I am at your service, Governor." As much as I hated this news, I respected Guo and his decision.

"I've heard stories of these men extending their power further than what's asked of them. I want you to keep an eye out on them, discreetly."

"You want me to police the Emperor's men? What about Yun?" I could feel my heart racing as I raised my voice. "If anyone deserves the honor, it's him!"

"Yun will remain my personal guard. These are the times when I will need him most. The Emperor's success was not due to benevolence."

I nodded to him in understanding. "As you wish."

The conversation helped piece my random memories together more clearly. As I walked out to the courtyard, yesterday's sparring session with Yun flowed into my mind.

I PACED AROUND THE DOJO, the sound of my steps dampened by the padding as I kept my eyes on Yun. Sweat dripped into his eyes and down his long, dark beard. His long braid caught the light as he pretended to rush at me, still full of vigor after several rounds of sparring.

"Want to make this interesting?" He laughed while picking up a wooden training sword, throwing it to me with little time to react. I caught it as he picked up his own and charged at me. I jumped to my side and swung, almost striking his arm. He had thrown his body forward at just the right moment to avoid my wooden blade.

He cracked a sly smirk. "Not as bad as last time." We found each other on opposite sides of the dojo now, still pacing each other.

"You know my blade work is sloppy!" I had been practicing, but I had a long way to go until I was on his level.

"This is the only way you'll get better. It might save your life someday!" His voice thundered through the room, far more vociferous than necessary.

We both took a few seconds to catch our breath and slowly inched closer to each other. He swung first, striking my blade as I parried the attack perfectly, to my surprise.

"Good!" His voice echoed loudly as he charged forward on the offensive. I blocked attack after attack, but with each block I felt my body weaken. He continued attacking relentlessly, with my entire body feeling the vibration of each clash. With each attack, I was pushed backwards, now leaving little room between my back and the wall.

I gasped for breath as I desperately tried to speak between the assaults. "Enough!" Yun's eyes radiated an intense look I had never seen before, which showed no signs of stopping the barrage.

Our blades met upright and stood still as we met face to face. I could feel his pressure on my blade as I pushed back with my remaining strength. It became more than I could handle and my grip loosened.

"You're going to need to learn how to fight if you want to take on the Royal Guard!" He shook his head and laughed.

I was filled with curiosity. "What are you talking about?" Just then, my arm wavered, giving him all he needed to thrust both swords towards my face. They fell towards me, surrounding my throat leaving me no room to move as they pinned me against the wall. He pushed his sword harder against my throat causing me to gasp for air.

"I don't know why he picked you, but you better learn fast. And if you ever even look at Lijuan the wrong way, pray I end you swiftly."

He held the blades tightly against me causing my airway to close. My head started pounding and I felt blood rush to my face. I tried to push the wooden blades away, but I was so weakened it was useless.

Time felt like it was standing still until he finally released his hold and backed away. Since I had been pushing against him, my body fell forward and lay limp on the dojo floor. My hands shot up to my neck as I coughed and gasped for air at the same time. I could see him looking down at me in the corner of my eye with a look of disappointment. He walked towards me and extended a hand. I reached out and he pulled me up fast and gazed into my eyes.

"You have to learn to fight for your life. Times are changing." He walked away slowly, leaving me alone looking back with confusion, out of breath.

3

———————

Lijuan was in the courtyard sitting by the pond, singing. Her beautiful song reminded me of the ones my mother would sing for me as a child in Japan, even with weeks of travel in between the two lands. I slowly walked closer, catching her attention after I stepped on a fallen tree branch making a loud crunch. She looked up and smiled but kept singing as if to me. She looked so perfect in the courtyard, surrounded by the colorful flowers and trees. The sun was setting fast, giving her eyes a twinkle that reminded me why I had fallen for her so long ago. I sat down next to her and she stopped singing, turning to face me with a beaming smile.

"Did you accept my father's request?" She innocently batted her eyes while smoothing out her gown.

"How long have you known?"

"Only a few days now. Father says they should be coming any day now. Are you worried?" She looked at me with a concerned look on her face.

"I'm confused, but I will do whatever I must to keep us safe."

"He keeps saying the Emperor means well and only wants to protect us, but the look in his eyes when he says it, he's worried about something." Her smile was nowhere in sight now. She looked out into the gardens and sighed heavily.

"He's worried they're replacing him soon. A regime change in the province."

"Is there anything we can do?" She turned to face me, expressing enough worry to break my heart.

I gripped her hands and let out a faint smile. "Be vigilant, for now."

A faint boom reverberated through the air, echoing off in the distance. We both sprang to our feet and turned in the noise's direction. In the distance, a small cloud of smoke billowed on the far end of the village.

Another small explosion followed, with the sounds of screaming and pounding. Yun ran from his quarters near the guest house followed by another of the Governor's guardsmen, both dressed in full leather battle armor.

"I think the barbarians are back!" Yun ran towards the gate with the other guard struggling to keep up with his stride. "Grab a sword from my room. I hope you've been paying attention, Hagaki!"

I told Lijuan to take her father to the mansion's cellar and lock the door until we returned. She nodded and gave me a quick kiss before running out the room. I hurried towards Yun's room, now in search of a weapon. The door to his room was wide open. A half-eaten bowl of noodles sat steaming on the table, which made me realize the danger looming. He took dinner almost as seriously as training. I glanced around the neatly organized room to find several weapons resting against his spare leather breastplate. The armor had seen better days, but I had no idea what I was getting into. I threw it over my tunic and grabbed the sharpest blade I could find.

I darted out of the room after Lijuan and her father slammed the main door shut, hopefully locking themselves from danger. Off in the distance, I heard the clash of steel against steel. Dark grey smoke rose from the fires spreading throughout the area. I drew closer towards the madness, passing a small hut burning rapidly. The bodies of several villagers lay lifeless around it. I looked away after I recognized a bar patron from last night on the ground, bloodied. Turning my head back to the noises, I spotted Yun and the other guard fending off blows from a small group of attackers.

Sweat and fear lingered in the air as six of the invaders circled around them. The attackers wore all black armor with hooded masks obscuring their identity. They had no defining markings, but I assumed they were the nearby barbarians who often attacked villagers traveling outside the safety of the province guard. One of the barbarians screamed a battle cry which seemed to signal a message to the other men. Not wanting to find out what that meant, I picked up my pace and rushed towards them.

Using surprise to my advantage and putting my pride aside, I thrust my sword into the back of an attacker. My aim was off, but I registered a clean hit through the thigh of the man who instantly collapsed, screaming in horror. I pulled my blade out, sending blood leaking down his leggings. He wailed in pain and dropped his weapon, grabbing the wound.

The scream distracted the other men, giving Yun a chance to launch a killing blow at the nearest barbarian. His attack connected, slicing across the man's neck, instantly felling him. The other guard was not as lucky and was hit in the chest by an attacker's mace. The force propelled him backwards until he slammed hard into the wall of a nearby hut, cracking its wall.

I jumped over to the guards aid but I was too late. Before I made it, his attacker swung the mace again, this time smashing against his skull. The guard jerked to the side from the impact and went limp as soon as the mace passed. Again, using surprise to my advantage, I swung my sword at his attacker's unarmored legs. The barbarian let out a howl as my blade passed through both ankles, spraying a red mist into the air.

I turned to see Yun's blade being removed from another of the invaders' chest, leaving only two of them. They slowly backed off after taking stock of the bodies around them. In the distance, a horn sounded.

I looked over to spot another hooded mask, this one in black atop an armored horse watching from a distance. The hood lowered his horn and picked up a bow from his side. With us in their sights, they set an arrow in the bow and aimed in our direction. The two barbarians sprinted away from us, towards the safety of the armored attacker. The arrow remained pointed at us—a silent warning not to follow.

I stood my ground, feeling somewhat accomplished that we had forced them to retreat, somewhat scared out of my mind that I'd get an arrow in the forehead. Yun, clearly not satisfied with letting them free, started after them. The masked attacker let go of his grip on the string and sent the arrow whistling through the air. Yun twisted toward his left to dodge the bolt but caught it in the shoulder. He shrieked in pain on the fall toward the ground. Not missing a beat, Yun made a feeble attempt to stand, but only managed to get to his knees. I could see the look of helplessness and rage build in his eyes. With one hand still grabbing the arrow in his shoulder, he slammed the other fist into the soil. I looked up to see the barbarians fade into the distance. The cowardly feeling inside me faded after I realized I would have joined Yun on the ground—or had a fate even worse. Trying not to let the what-if scenarios play out in my head, I ran over to Yun and put my hand under his good arm to help him up. To my surprise, he did not refuse my help and stood strong with his head high.

We walked together towards Master Shen's house, whose knowledge of herbs had saved my life more than once. We left the battle scene, thankful that the fire in the hut behind us appeared to be dying down. A few other villagers ran out to check on the others involved in the battle, but it did not sound like the fallen had survived the attack.

4

———

Master Shen opened his door cautiously and peered out. He studied me for a moment, worried that the battle had come to his door. In a way it did, I suppose. He looked deep in my eyes for a moment and then down at Yun. The door instantly opened and Shen motioned for us to come in.

I helped seat Yun on the closest chair to the door and thanked Shen for letting us in.

Shen walked over and inspected Yun's wound closely. "The arrow is in there pretty good." He shook his head in disapproval as he began cutting away at the clothing near it. "But I believe there is hope yet."

Shen opened a cupboard filled with all sorts of medicines and carefully pondered the selection. He grabbed two small vials and proceeded to pour them together into a ceramic mug. He mixed them gently, making a thick greyish syrup that had a strong medicinal odor. Shen returned to us and handed the concoction to Yun.

"Drink." It was an order, not a request.

Yun took the cup and drank without hesitation. Within a few seconds, Yun lowered his head, from either the pain or the effects of the drink. Shen left the room briefly and returned with some candles and a small basket. I took a quick look in the basket to see it contained a few herbs and roots, and a small but lethally sharp blade.

Shen walked around the room and began to light the small candles. Each candle made a quiet hiss when lit. A strong sulfur smell filled the room causing my eyes to water.

The healer turned to me and spoke with authority, "This may take a few hours, but I will take care of him. He won't be awake for most of this as I fear the pain alone could kill him. It looks close to his heart, I will need to be very precise."

I nodded in understanding, realizing that this would be a very delicate procedure and he needed his full concentration. As I left Shen's hut, I felt a sharp pulsing in my side. I was so caught up in helping Yun that I hadn't realized I was injured myself. The adrenaline from the fight must have blocked the pain emanating from the small gash near my lower abdomen. Now that the adrenaline had faded, I found myself battling to ignore it. Instead of turning around and going back to Shen for help, I decided it was more important to check on Lijuan and her father. And I convinced myself he couldn't spare a minute being focused on Yun.

I made it about half way into the courtyard when my face started to swell with heat. Each step I took forward felt like I was hiking upwards and my boots were lined with lead. Sweat poured down my face and neck. I looked down to see a bright red stain near the wound. The world around me swirled, slowly at first but quickly picking up speed. I closed my eyes for just a moment which threw me completely off balance. I crashed down into the brick-lined garden and heard a voice scream out my name from the distance.

I OPENED my eyes and was surrounded by almost complete darkness. My entire body ached and my mouth felt it was coated in the kind of disgusting film you get when you're dehydrated. I clawed around my sides to discover I was on the plush bed inside the Governor's guest house. A burning sensation shot over my body that emanated from my lower side. I felt around the area to find it had been bandaged and sealed with a sticky substance that butterflied the wound together.

The thirst was so unbearable I decided my next task was to get some water in me. This normally simple task felt impossible. After several minutes of stalling, I gathered all my energy and placed my feet on the floor next to the bed. I pushed up with my remaining strength and managed to stand—albeit shaky. Walking towards the door, I heard a loud commotion outside my window. I blocked it out of my head and continued on my quest to quench the thirst. I made it to the door and pulled at the handle. The wooden door felt like a sheet of steel in my weakened state. My second attempt to open the door was much more successful, but as it flew open my arm dropped limp. I shook off the numbness and continued outside to the courtyard where I knew I'd find the pond waiting for me. Listen, at this point I would have drank from almost anything. I hobbled to the pond and plopped down on its ledge. My hands dove towards the water, splashing it all over my face like I had just found an oasis in the desert.

Finally satisfied, I realized the noise was even louder in the courtyard. It sounded like a happy commotion so I used the ledge as leverage to push myself up. I headed out towards the gates praying that I was right.

There was a large bonfire in the center of the village with dozens surrounding it cheering and celebrating. Some wore colorful ceremonial garb, some were singing, others dancing. It was hard to make much out since my eyes were still adjusting to the bright fire and moonlight. Fumbling forward, I squinted to see who I thought was the Governor holding a glass of wine.

I stumbled closer towards the fire with my weak legs already hoping for their next rest. Lijuan noticed me approaching and called out excitedly. "Hagaki!" She hurried over and gave me a tight hug, then planted a quick kiss on my cheek. The force of her embrace knocked me off balance and I could tell she was using all her strength to right me. "Sorry! I'm so happy to see you up!"

"Quite a celebration you're having here." My voice was raspy, still raw from the deep sleep.

"I was going to wake you, but I thought you needed the sleep. I've been checking up on you every other hour."

"What happened?" I coughed.

"Master Shen says it looks like one of those barbarian's caught you in the side. He patched you up after you collapsed in front of the mansion. You've been out a whole day, sleepy!" She looked relieved. "I'm so glad you're well, Hagaki."

"Thank you Lijuan." I managed a smile and cleared my throat. "I feel—weak. How is Yun holding up?"

"Yun is with the crowd, celebrating with my father." She pointed back towards the bonfire. "He was up on his feet as soon as he woke up from Shen's cocktail." She shot me a wry smile. "The idiot doesn't know when to quit."

We both laughed. My abdomen pulsed with pain, reminding me that laughter might not always be the best medicine.

"What's the celebration for anyways?"

"We're celebrating the lives of all lost recently and—" Her frown became a soft smile. "You silly!"

I couldn't have timed it better myself, at that very moment the Governor noticed me. "And if it isn't our other hero himself, Hagaki!" he announced, waving to me.

All eyes turned toward me. The villagers erupted with more cheering as I walked closer to the celebration with Lijuan at my side. A small "Hagaki" chant started which brought a huge smile to my blushing face. Yes, I blushed. I stood near the edge of the party and waved to the villagers, greeting the ones closest to me.

"What are you doing over there? Come here and address the village!" the Governor shouted over the cheers.

I looked around the fire to see the smiling faces of the

villagers still looking at me. Next to the Governor, Yun stood proudly. He waved me over with his free arm, the other tied close to his chest in a crude sling. I walked next to them and faced my audience. The cheering quieted, giving me the ground to talk.

I cleared my throat and faced the crowd. "I thank you deeply for the cheers and praise. Even though many of our attackers fled or were killed, we must not lose sight of us as a people. We lost a lot of friends recently," I took a moment to lock eyes with everyone watching. "And while you cheer my name I ask you to please celebrate in memory of them."

I bowed and walked away leaving the crowd silent. Their noise level soon rose after Yun raised his glass as a toast at me. I smiled back and sat on a rock near the fire.

Despite having the Governor's blessings and friendship, after hearing the village cheer my name, I felt like I had finally earned respect in my new home. I smiled to myself, but I tried to hide it fast after my solemn speech. As amazing as it felt to be the local hero, in addition to being celebrated, I felt like it would be disrespectful not to remember the dead.

I was surprised to see Yun sitting next to me by the fire. I must have been deep in thought not to notice him so close. He looked over at me realizing that I had just noticed he was there. "Did you notice anything odd about those men, Hagaki?" Yun sat motionless, intently waiting for my response.

I nodded. "Their armor. I've only seen the barbarians on two or three occasions but they never wore anything like those men who attacked us."

Yun took a deep sigh. "You are correct. I investigated their bodies after I recovered. They were wearing black chain armor. I could imagine one or two of them equipped with this type of armor if they stole it from some rich travelers." He looked over at some villagers celebrating and then back at the fire. "But for a fleet of them to be fully armored in matching chain, this is alarming to say the least."

"Then how are we to believe that they were just common barbarians? Maybe guard from another town?"

"Our province is unified, Hagaki. We haven't been at war with any neighboring villages in ages. No, under the armor these bodies had dirt, grit, and their skin was tattooed with common nomadic symbols." His face matched the concern in his voice. He took a sip from his glass and savored the taste for a moment until he was brought back to the present. "They fought like barbarians too, there is no mistaking this. Except they rarely attack in broad daylight like this."

"I don't understand what you're getting at. So the drifters got their hands on armor and it went to their head. They aren't diplomatic and war is all they know." I knew I was coming off as defensive. In the back of my mind I had a good idea of what he was implying, but I tried to convince myself he was wrong.

"War and money. They were given that armor, it's obvious. Most likely heavy coin to go along with it as well. As for the rider that shot me with that arrow—" He glanced down at his wounded shoulder and then back to me. "No barbarian has aim like that. Let alone do they have any sort of battle plan. Whenever I've dealt with them, it's to the death. Retreat is a foreign term to them."

"So the horse rider was their benefactor?" I waited timidly like a small child barely grasping a concept. In my defense I was still a bit groggy from the long sleep.

"Yes. Barbarians are not prone to make deals like this, so the incentive must have been good. I have no doubt they will turn on their supplier once their agreement is settled. If not sooner."

"Who do you think is behind all this? The Governor did seem very concerned about the Emperor's direct intervention in this area."

"You're smarter than you let on, Hagaki." He shook his head giving me the impression he was annoyed, before his lips curled into a smile. "You were already thinking the same thing as me the whole time, weren't you?"

Our nervous laughter died down fast once the reality sank in. I stared at the flickering fire for a moment trying not to think of what might be looming on the horizon.

"Hagaki!" the Governor shouted, breaking my train of thought.

I turned, seeing he was still celebrating gleefully. He held up the lute I saw earlier in my room and smiled brightly. My head instantly filled with years of knowledge playing the instrument. Notes and techniques swirled inside my head like a tornado causing me to brace down on the rock for a split second.

"Play for us!"

I walked over and grabbed the lute. I instantly positioned it in a way that felt natural to me. My fingers ran through the strings. Without hesitating, my fingers went to work. The instrument erupted with beautiful music that matched the tone of the celebration. Instinctively I started to sing, following the tone and melody. I performed for what seemed like an hour until my fingers were numb. Looking around the crowd, only a few remained standing and swaying to my music. The crowd had thinned now, hours deep in the night. Several villagers lay sleeping near the fire while a few others looked like they were deciding whether to lie down on the ground or try to make it to their bed.

I put my lute down and bowed to the small crowd. I scanned the area and found no trace of Yun or the Governor. Lijuan was still in the audience, curled up on the ground in a fetal position sleeping soundly. I crouched down to her and ran my fingers through her hair, waking her gently. She smiled and nestled into me for a moment before opening her eyes.

I had finally let myself relax, melting with her in the stillness of the night and ignoring the looming fear of what was to come for our village.

INTERLUDE, DETROIT

So as it turned out, I've always had music in my blood. Back in China, my lute was only second to my blade. But back in the United States, my rap career soared way above my swordsmanship. To be fair, it was years since I picked up a blade. Although I've been told it's like riding a bike. They probably meant motorcycle.

A lot of things are hard to explain. I don't mean this as a slight to anyone, but we're trained to accept certain things as fact from an early age. And my life is one of those things that goes against some of what you may believe.

Many religions have teachings on reincarnation. The soul being born in a new body. For ease, this concept is the only thing that's helped make sense of my life. Lives? But from most of what I've read, remembering the past typically isn't part of the process.

At first, life in the twenty-first century was as normal as could be. Born and briefly raised in Poland, I immigrated to the United States at an early age. As the years went on, my childhood became a bit hazy at times, like some thoughts were trying to break through but just quite couldn't. I figure my mind actively blocked my previous life to protect me from seeing anything I wouldn't be ready for. Imagine a three-year-old seeing himself fighting barbarians in vivid detail. I don't think the adults in my life would understand if I were to tell them. And it would derail any sense of normal childhood development. Plus it was a great way to ease my ancient warrior self into the twenty-first century. I can only imagine attacking cars and being baffled by the simplest things like electricity or a radio.

In my later teen years, the memories broke through. I look at them as being 'Unlocked' for lack of a better word. It's one of those things that is hard to explain without experiencing it. At first they came as dreams. Vivid, shocking dreams which led me to process and assimilate memories into my psyche gradually, until I realized my true past.

I still don't have all the details of my life back in Ancient China. Sometimes I wonder if my past is being shown to me when it's necessary. Other times I think it's all random. Either way, what I know of the past seems to correlate to my age, slowly unlocking more memories as I get older. Another point for the theory of the timing being intentional. The idea of seeing my death is still scary. I could see why I wouldn't want to know that now.

There's still enough that haunts me, keeping me up at night. Despite the existential dread, I've found some peace and even benefited. With my lives connected directly, I never stopped learning. Hundreds of years apart, I share a unique bond to the past. Whether it was looking into the mirror or a reflection in a pond, I knew it was me, no matter the exterior. Plus my eyes have always had an eerie glow to them. Not a special power, but quite a few have got lost in them. It comes in handy. And even though there wasn't as much fighting in the future, my past gave me a giant head start in my career.

5

W hile most American twenty-one-year olds celebrate their birthday with their first legal drink in a bar, I set off to California in hopes of becoming famous. In retrospect, it's kind of funny how spontaneous I had been about the whole thing. I didn't really have a specific occupation or goal in mind, I just thought it would be interesting to be seen. Three days before my birthday, I grabbed my guitar and a backpack of clothes and jumped on a greyhound bus.

During the trip, I didn't even think about what I'd do when I got to California. I spent a good deal of the first half gazing out the window with a childlike curiosity, just taking it all in. There were quite a few stops on the way from Detroit to San Diego, with people coming and going during the layovers, but most of them kept to themselves. Even though the bus was pretty spacious, a day of being cooped up took its toll. After sleeping through most of the rest stops, I decided to take advantage of the layover in Salt Lake City.

The driver announced we had a full hour before we'd get moving again so I set the alarm on my Timex. I jumped off the bus onto a dirt trail in between the large truck stop that doubled as a bus station. After remaining still for so long, I figured the best option was to shock my body awake to feel a bit more alive. My legs almost buckled under me, weak from sitting so long in my chair. I caught my balance and launched into a full sprint down the path. My heart started beating fast and blood rushed throughout my body. I felt like I was shaking cobwebs from my head as I dashed further down the path into a lightly wooded area. I stayed parallel to the freeway, making sure I'd be able to find my way back.

My run through the small plot of nature gave me a sense of freedom, away from all the industrialization and chaos. Again, not easy to explain, but even though I had been living in the 21st century for a while now, occasionally I longed for open spaces. I now realize that this was the longing for something that I had back in China. Writing this even now, I have to remind myself I had made peace with that chapter of my life long ago. If I didn't look at each phase as a new journey, I would be stuck with regret and dwell on the past, which would get me nowhere fast.

My Timex beeped reminding me that the 25 minute timer was up. I instantly turned around and headed back in the same direction I came from, towards the truck stop. My legs propelled me even faster, showing no signs of letting up. I've always wondered if more than my experiences followed me into this life. Like everything fused as a whole, enhancing some of my abilities. Stronger than I should be, faster than I should be. Not superhuman by any means, but I've always had an edge in certain things. Just a theory, though.

I made it to the bus with ten minutes to spare. About a dozen passengers were lined up by the door waiting to get checked back on. I realized I had some extra time, so I walked over to the convenience store connected to the truck stop. The old lady at the register waved me in without raising her head. Her eyes were glued on a small TV near the counter broadcasting what sounded like pro wrestling.

I grabbed a bottle of chocolate milk and a granola bar and headed to the register. In my peripheral, I noticed a twenty something brunette stuffing various things in her purse. She looked around to see if anyone noticed and caught my eyes fixed on her. To be honest, I wasn't staring because she was shoplifting. Maybe it was the fact I'd been pressed against a greyhound window for 32 hours straight or the way she wore her hip hugging black jeans and a size too small Power Rangers shirt. She seemed to have a glow about her. Her shoulder length hair looked kind of frizzy, like she'd left the house right after a shower. Her fading green and purple streaks matched the purple eyeshadow, lightly sparkling whenever she turned her head. At around six feet, she was roughly two inches taller than me, the boots probably giving her a lift.

I got the impression that she thought herself quite the rebel. I'm not happy to admit it, but I stereotyped her. I figured from her Punky Brewster exterior that she was the kind of girl most guys would get shy around in a bar.

The sort that had the strong and silent vibe surrounding her. But the look I saw in her eyes when I caught her, it was like I saw straight through all the defenses she'd put up.

I'd seen plenty of beautiful girls in my life, but something seemed different about this one. I felt drawn to her, like a magnetic energy was pulling me closer. Comfortable and familiar, yet foreign.

She turned away and sank back behind an aisle. Partially in view, I saw her chest rapidly rise and fall. If I hadn't been sure if she was stealing, there was no doubt now. She popped her head up for a few seconds and caught my eyes a second time. I smiled and winked before heading back to the cashier. The woman at the register mastered the skill of keeping her eye on the television while ringing up my items—I was impressed. I walked back outside to see that the line had died down and most of the passengers were back on the bus.

The driver checked my ID and commented as most people do. "Your hair looks different in a ponytail." He squinted as he held the license up next to my face. "Looks much darker too."

I faked a pleasant smile which seemed enough for him and climbed aboard the bus. I was happy to see that the seat next to me was still empty. I thought about what the driver said and realized that before the run I had tied my shoulder length hair back. Even in the dirty window's reflection, my normally pale complexion had more color in it. I ran my fingers through my hair, still wet with sweat causing it to appear a darker brown than usual.

I set my backpack on the empty seat next to me and drank my milk in a matter of seconds. Before closing my eyes, I took a bite of the granola bar and rested my head on the chilly glass window. I felt my head sink down low while the bus engine purred to life, easing me to sleep.

6

———————

A stiff bump in the road jolted me hard against the window. Disoriented, my eyes shot open to blinding sunlight—adding to the confusion. One hand went over my eyes, and the other to my head where the sharp throbbing was.

"Are you okay?" a soft female voice next to me asked. I lowered my head toward the voice, looking for something soft, like a dog nestling into a pillow.

"I'm. Ughh. It hurts!" I must have sounded like a bratty kid.

I realized my head was flush against a woman's shoulder. She was warm and offered just the right amount of support. Still waking up, my first reaction was to lie against her for a while—I was comfortable. But after a few seconds the confusion passed. I tore my head away and looked up to see the girl from the gas station. She felt more muscular than I imagined, now being up close.

She batted her long dark lashes. "Hey there."

"It was my first reaction, sorry."

She had a cute laugh and was even prettier up close. Her green eyes sparkled innocently back at me. Or maybe it was her makeup, either way I wanted to put my head back down and go to sleep but resisted.

"You match way too well," I said, still groggy from being torn out of a dream. Not the smoothest thing to come out of my mouth but even I have been tongue tied.

"Huh?" She definitely wasn't expecting that.

"Your hair and your eyes, your makeup. You look so, coordinated," I said, with a stutter. I debated why I continued with the ridiculous topic.

"Wowww," she smirked. "That has to be the nicest-worst compliment I've ever gotten!"

I let out an embarrassed laugh and shook my head. I was probably blushing. "I'm sorry, I don't usually wake up in pure shock!"

"You must have hit your head pretty hard, huh?"

"Let's start over." I reached out my hand in an overly friendly way. "I'm Jay. I usually go by Hagaki."

So as I was getting at earlier, I've gone by a few names. Hagaki was a nickname I remember going by after I arrived in China that carried over to this life. While not having any outward characteristics of my Japanese self, I felt the nickname helped bridge my lives and stuck with it, despite the confusion it caused. And in some situations, it was easier than using my Polish surname.

She had a curious squint then took my hand, playing along just as jokingly as me. "Nice to meet you, Mister Hagaki. My name is Olivia."

Our overly exaggerated handshake was even more

awkward—sitting side-by-side didn't leave much room. My smile must have beamed just as much as hers.

"So, do you normally sit down next to sleeping strangers?" I joked playfully.

"Nah, it's something new I'm trying. Part of my therapy is to be more spontaneous." Her voice was laced with sarcasm. "Plus, you're kind of cute." She was playing along. I was starting to like her even more. "Hey wait a minute!" She furrowed her eyebrows and pursed her lips softly. "Aren't we starting over?"

"Too late for that now," I said, with a goofy smile. "So, I don't remember you getting on the bus."

"I really wanted that granola bar you had. By the way, it was delicious." I exaggerated a laugh and cocked my head at her, intently looking in her direction. I really wanted an answer.

She exhaled softly, looking down to her fingers nervously circling a ripped patch of fabric on her seat. "I wanted to do something drastic. I was deciding whether to take the bus or just try shoplifting. Maybe even get caught just because, but that old fart at the gas station was in a world of her own." Her cheeks became a light pinkish color. She looked up to meet my eyes and the tension in her jaw and cheeks eased. I swear it has to be my eyes. People seem to trust me within minutes of meeting me.

She looked away and focused straight ahead at the driver. "I was only half joking about the spontaneous thing. Up until last month I'd played my life so straight. To the point that I just got sick of it. Sick of even waking up. Sick of surrounding myself with people who pretend to be friends."

"Rich girl, controlling dad?" It was crass but I couldn't hold back.

"Rich girl, no dad. But thanks for trying to stereotype me." Her tone didn't change. I wondered if she was offended or not. "I saw a therapist for a couple of months and she helped me open up more. Told me to take a vacation. Take some... chances. Try doing something you normally wouldn't. I guess I take things seriously."

For a split second I got a creepy vibe from her, I won't lie. She was coming on strong by opening to me so fast and, as far as I knew, it sounded like she followed me on this bus without knowing who I was. But I thought I could hear the truth in her voice. She was hurting and was searching for something new in life. I reminded myself that not everyone wants to hide or bottle their emotions like I had for so long. Maybe she really did want to just talk to a stranger. Or she was the best god damned liar I'd ever heard in my hundred plus years of combined experience on this earth.

The bus still had a few hours until we arrived, so I played along, trying to keep the conversation light. "Why California?"

"I could ask you the same thing." There was a hint of annoyance in her voice. I realized she was spilling her soul and was looking for more.

"Make a name for myself. Booked the trip on a whim. Figured it's worth a shot."

Her lips turned upwards to an innocent smile. "There's probably a lot I could learn from you."

"More than you'll ever know—" I said, quietly under my breath.

She sat there looking at me, squinting her eyes like she was studying my tone. After a few seconds, she flashed a teeth baring smile. "You're an interesting man, Hagaki." She yawned and stretched her arms and legs. "But just because I think you're cute doesn't mean you can try any funny business, mister."

She turned the other direction and rested her head against the chair cushion. In the reflection, I saw her eyes close and she fell into deep sleep almost instantly. I had a strange feeling about that girl, but it was definitely the good kind of strange. She was funny, attractive, and maybe as lost as me.

The bus rumbled softly as it glided down the seemingly endless stretch of desert. I looked out the window and felt a chill from the unknown. My eyes grew heavier with each passing freeway sign. I began to slouch, falling back into the same position—against the window.

7

———

The next time I woke was much less abrupt. I looked out the window and saw we were parked at the San Diego Terminal. A few passengers were still exiting and getting their suitcases from the cubby areas underneath the bus. I yawned and turned to look around the bus. The seat next to me was empty. I looked down at a crinkled note on the cushion.

Thanks for the chat, blue eyes.
Good luck making a name.
Maybe I'll see ya around?
-Liv

I put the note in my pocket and stood up and stretched my legs. I was the last person on the bus. The bus driver was cleaning their area and looked startled when noticing my reflection in the window. I apologized and gathered up my things.

"No big deal son, there's at least one every trip. At

least I didn't have to use the stick." With a smile, he motioned to the long wooden baton affixed over the windshield.

I faked a chuckle and grabbed my backpack, trying to get off the bus as fast as I could. I got the impression the driver was just a lonely old guy wanting to talk, but I had Hollywood waiting for me. After grabbing my guitar from underneath the storage area, I began my walk. After a few hours of walking, my stomach rumbled loudly. I had been so distracted by the unfamiliar sights that I had neglected to eat. My stomach directed me to a small diner off the main road.

For a greasy spoon, Arthur's Diner was well maintained and very clean, but it had that unmistakable oily smell in the air. I walked past the Please Be Seated sign toward a booth near the back corner. I positioned my guitar upright as my guest and plopped down across from it, facing the door. Ever since that particularly nasty incident in China a few (hundred) years ago, I've made sure to keep an eye on the door.

A young blond waitress wearing an old 1950s style uniform approached me almost immediately. With a bubbly personality and a slightly southern twang in her voice, she greeted me, "Hey there handsome, my name is Melissa and I'll be your waitress. Can I start you off with something to drink or an appetizer?"

"Handsome? I've been stuck on a bus without showering for over three days." I let out a soft chuckle. "Black Coffee. And a Chicken Caesar salad, light dressing."

She giggled and nodded. "And for your friend there?" She motioned toward my guitar.

"Oh, I think she's good for now, thanks!"

As she jotted down my order on her notepad, her lips curled into a warm smile. "She, huh?" Melissa put the pen in her apron and headed back towards the kitchen.

I looked around the nearly empty diner, trying to overhear some of the other conversations. An elderly couple a few booths away were talking about one of their friends' funeral arrangements. There was a young couple that appeared to be on their first date sitting at a small table. I couldn't hear what they were saying, but I saw lots of blushing, playing with hair, and awkward eye contact. Young love, so cute.

You'd think I'd be somewhat of a Casanova being alive as long as I have. Even with my extra decades of knowledge, I've always found something new to learn about the complexities of human relationships.

At the counter furthest from me sat an older man in a grey tweed suit. He must have come in after me since I didn't notice him when I first arrived. Out of the corner of my eye, I caught him looking in my direction from time to time. It was a little unsettling after the third or fourth time, but I realized I may have seemed out-of-place being on a date with a guitar, after all.

Melissa came back with my salad and coffee and then sat next to the guitar. I had started chomping away without noticing she was sitting across from me.

"So," she said. "Where ya from?"

I tried to respond but my mouth was full. I chewed a bit more and swallowed. That was never an easy question to answer, at least honestly.

"Bussed in from Detroit. Another wide-eyed kid trying to make it big."

"I've definitely heard that one before." Her southern accent was shining through.

"I thought I'd spare you the details."

"Hey, every story is different." She rested her elbows on the table and leaned in closer. "No matter how similar they start."

"You've heard a lot, I take it?" I took a sip of the coffee and realized how awful it tasted chasing the salad.

She smiled, reminiscing about the last year she had spent in California, a stark contrast to the comfort of Houston, her childhood home. "Still get as lost as a tourist some days. What're your plans, hun?"

"Hmmm, does drifting around town count as a plan?"

"You boys are worse than the gals! You at least need a place to stay while you find a day job." She pulled a business card from her pocket and handed it to me. "This place is pretty cheap and has weekly rates. It's a hole in the wall, but unless you come from money, it's your best bet."

In my past life, I ended up doing well for myself. But unfortunately, I didn't have a 401k back in China. This life was a fresh start as far as my possessions go. If only I had a couple of coins from back then, I could make a mint.

"Melissa!" a voice barked out from the kitchen. "Break's over!"

I took the card and thanked her before she got up and hurried to the back. After finishing the salad, I took a look at the bill. She didn't charge me for the coffee. What a doll. I picked up a pen and drew an outline of the state of Texas with a crude bell in the middle of it. Under it, I wrote 'Southern Bell (that's you)'. I slipped a few extra dollars as my tip and headed outside. With my guitar and backpack in tow, I was ready to take on the city.

Until I stepped outside and realized how late it was. Looking back in the diner, I saw only the young couple remained. The bank across the street had an LED marquee that showed it was now after 9 pm. I decided I'd take Melissa's advice and check out the motel. It also helped that it was on the same street and I didn't know the area at all. I continued, counting down the building numbers to make sure I was headed in the right direction.

I figured it would be close, but it was a good twenty-minute walk until I arrived at the motel. From the outside, it looked like your average dumpy spot. The flickering vacancy sign matched the other lights flashing above the room numbers—at least the ones that still had them.

I walked into the small lobby and was greeted by a large sweaty man in a flannel shirt that was opened too generously for my liking. He muttered something when he saw me walk in, taking his eyes off a monitor under the desk.

He yanked an unlit half-burnt cigar out of his mouth and grumbled, "How can I help you, kid?"

"I'd like a room, just a night please." I put the card from Melissa on the counter.

He looked down at it and nodded. "Thirty bucks, no room service. Stay the week, it's one-fifty."

I pulled the money from my pocket and handed it

over to him. His sweaty fingers grabbed it surprisingly fast and in the same motion, he threw me a pair of keys. They grazed my fingers and dropped to the floor.

"Work on your reflexes, kid. This town will eat you." His eyes went back down to the monitor, acting like I had already walked out the door.

As I bent down to pick them up, I noticed the number 14, barely visible from years of wear and tear. I looked back at the manager, still glued to the monitor, and shook my head as I walked out. Room 14 was on the second level of the motel complex. I was one of the lucky ones with a light; ever so dim above the door. I put the key in the door and pushed in. The door opened before I even turned the key. Awesome.

I flicked on the light switch upon entering the room but it remained just as dark as it was before.

"Perfect," I said under my breath. I felt my way around the room, using only the moonlight to guide me. The air inside was stale and had the faint odor of a citrus cleaning solution. I found my way to the bathroom and felt for the switch. This one actually worked, giving me a good look. It was in much better shape than I expected, but I had been expecting the worst. It was on par with a gas station bathroom that was cleaned once, maybe twice a week. Plus, it had a tub that doubled as a shower, no curtain.

The bathroom light allowed me to see my way around the bedroom. I turned on the bedside lamp and laid on the mattress, looking up at the ceiling. The bed squeaked a bit as I settled in, but it was surprisingly soft despite the rugged appearance. Suddenly feeling a wave of sleepiness pass over me, I decided I would clean myself up tomorrow and closed my eyes.

The bedside phone rang loudly, ripping me away from my dreams. I turned over to see the alarm clock read 4:00 AM next to the phone on the nightstand. My eyes were still adjusting to the moonlight in the room, causing me to completely misjudge the distance of the phone as I reached for it. I fell out of the bed hard, making a loud thud. The phone stopped ringing while I gathered myself and stood back up groggily.

8

I looked up to find I had unknowingly drifted off with the door ajar. All my belongings were in place and thankfully no one else had decided to join me. Making sure the door was now properly closed *and* locked, I now saw the rest of the room. Faded blue shag carpeting covered the floor, with enough stains to rival the designs in an abstract painting. The walls were painted white, at least once before. They now had a dull grey coat that chipped away at all the corners and various areas. The ceiling had a nice yellow tint to it from years of trapped cigarette smoke.

My queen sized bed had a beautiful lime-green comforter over it that matched the rest of the outdated decor. I glanced around the small room noting the dresser, table, and the most exciting thing of all, the mini fridge.

Still angry from the random wake up call, I decided to take a shower since I was awake and as alert as I could be —at least without a cup of coffee. I cleaned myself up the best I could in the tepid shower water and trimmed my beard in front of the dirty, cracked mirror. As I finished dressing, I spotted the sun beginning to rise through the dusty drapes in the window.

I grabbed my guitar and looked back at the room with a small smile. I had a good feeling I would be calling it home for quite a while. Despite its condition, compared to a lot of other places I had stayed in my life, it was a luxury suite. I'd had the chance to see the highest highs, and unfortunately, the lowest lows.

I walked around the city for a good hour before I found my destination, Silverlight Recording Studios. It wasn't the biggest in the business, but it sure was the closest. Earlier in the morning I had decided I'd try to get noticed the old-fashioned way—playing music on the street. Plus, I figured I could get a few dollars out of it. It definitely didn't hurt that the studio was next to a bank.

I found a corner a few buildings from the studio and set up shop. I fished an old baseball cap out of my backpack and threw it down in front of me. It was still early in the morning, but there was enough traffic on the street to be seen and heard. The grand plan was to catch a notable executive or agent on their way to work. I played for six hours that first day, only taking one bathroom break.

By the time I had finished playing, I had seventeen whole dollars in my hat—half paying my lunch and dinner. I came back to play for a few more hours, but the street was less crowded and much less giving. Eventually I got sleepy and walked back to the motel. I only had enough money left for two weeks, so I decided to pay a day at a time. The sweaty owner said something about me being a dime a dozen or something equally discouraging and gave me lucky number 14 again.

I made it up to my room exhausted. Normally I'd be able to function with just a few hours of sleep, but I was not used to the heat of California. And the jet-lag, or bus-lag, of being in a different time zone had my sleep all sorts of messed up. I set down my things and collapsed on the bed.

I was in the middle of rescuing Lijuan when a loud ringing rained from the heavens waking me up. I instantly sat forward in bed, covered in a cold sweat. Turning to the nightstand, I saw it was 4:00 AM again. This time, I reached the phone without falling.

"Hello?" I asked into the receiver.

There was a light static buzz on the other end of the line. I waited a few seconds before repeating myself. Nothing but static replied. I heard a loud click and the line went dead. I hit the star-sixty-something number to dial back the jerk that called me. It rang three times before playing a pre-recorded message. "I'm sorry, but the number you are calling has been disconnected."

"Fucking great," I said to myself. Tired of having my sleep interrupted, I felt around behind the nightstand and yanked the phone cord from the wall. I settled back in, fighting to find a comfortable position. I tossed and turned for a few hours until seeing the sun outside my window. I got myself ready and headed out for another day of playing. Before I started my walk to the studio, I stopped in at the motel lobby.

Inside the lobby, the motel manager sat with his eyes still glued to the monitor. A slight shiver went through my spine thinking how disgusting of a life it must be to sit and wait at that perch for all eternity. I pushed back my feelings and approached the counter.

"Hello, I'm the guy in room 14."

After a short pause, he finally turned to face me. "Lucky you." His gaze went back to the screen.

"I'm wondering about the phone in there—"

He cut me off without breaking his gaze from the screen. "Don't work. Lines in room twelve through seventeen hasn't worked in over a year, kid."

The look of pure confusion fell over my face. I scratched my beard for a second.

"Uh, no. That's not what I'm here for. Someone has been calling me in the middle of the night. Two nights in a row now."

He turned away from the TV to face me again, mouth agape. His lit cigar fell out of his mouth and onto his lap.

"Fuck!" He jumped up and batted the cigar away from his crotch. A second later, he bent to grab it from the ground and put it out on his desk. He settled back in his chair and acted like nothing happened. "Damn things'll kill ya. Now what'd you say kid?"

"The phone in my room, someone's been calling me at night," I repeated, clearly annoyed.

He lowered his head and squinted, studying me intently before shrugging. "The phone's been dead for a while, son. Phone company gave me some techno mumbo jumbo and said it's not possible for those lines to work anymore. Been meaning to have new lines ran through, but it's on my to-do list, ha ha."

"Well, mine is definitely working, and it's annoying

the hell out of me."

"Tell you what kid, I'll call the phone company and see what's what. Come back later."

I nodded and left, hoping it wasn't just a bullshit line he fed me so he could get back to his TV. He seemed more interested in his monitor than the motel or his wellbeing.

I resumed my trek to the same street as yesterday, still hoping someone from the studio would hear me playing. The walk was a bit easier after finding a shortcut across a few blocks. I moved one building closer to the studio hoping to increase my chances of being noticed.

I played for just under four hours but the time slipped away fast. Just like when I played the lute years before, I was able to find myself completely lost in the music. While the lute is similar to the guitar, both have their unique sound and feel. The first time I picked up a guitar in my second set of teen years, I immediately had a bond with the instrument. Music was natural to me in a way that was very comforting.

After graduating high school, I enrolled in a local community college and took a few music courses. They bored me, offering me little to no more knowledge I had gained on my own. I took a few other courses in various subjects that were slightly more informative, but I again became tired of reading instead of doing. I had a wealth of experience from my past, which made me a bit arrogant, thinking I could only learn so much from a classroom. I dropped out of college after my third semester. After that, I decided that I would continue learning using the hands-on approach.

I noticed it was starting to get dark so I began my last song. Stealing a glance into my collection hat, I counted about fifteen dollars in bills and change. During my last song of the night, I added my own rhyming lyrics to the simple rhythm. It had always been difficult for me to concentrate on playing while singing so in this case I deeply focused on watching my finger work.

"Beautiful music as ever, Hagaki," an unearthly voice said as it passed.

My focus was solely on the music, causing the words to take some time to register. My fingers stopped moving as soon as I realized I had just heard my name. I looked up and around me in search of the stranger to find an empty street.

Taking that as a sign I should get going, I packed my guitar and grabbed my hat. Looking inside, I saw a strange paper along with the rest of the day's earnings. I pulled out the paper to look at it closer. Faded, with slightly different dimensions than the rest of the money in my hat, the words Bank of England jumped out at me.

I shoved the money in my pockets and sprinted towards the stranger. More empty streets. So many questions filled my head with no real answers. I decided I would stop in at Arthur's Diner for a quick bite. Truthfully I was hoping that Melissa was there for some conversation. I was already beginning to get lonely and my motel manager wasn't exactly the best listener. Even though I didn't talk to her much, Melissa might know what I was going through. And she was pretty easy on the eyes.

9

———

Arthur's was just as slow as the last time I had visited. I walked in and sat down at the same booth, again setting my guitar across from me. When in a new place, I find making your own silly little traditions right away makes it feel more like home. Try it sometime.

This time, I decided I would actually read the menu. Nothing out of the ordinary, but the hamburger combo was the cheapest full meal I could find.

"Well, if it isn't my favorite couple!" Melissa said as she set a cup of black coffee in front of me.

I looked down at the coffee and back up at her. "Does this mean I'm a regular?"

"Nah, just a good tipper," she said with a smile. "Plus that thang you do with the guitar is super cute."

I shrugged and motioned to my wooden guest. "She's the money maker right now." I took a sip of coffee, bitter as ever.

She looked over to the kitchen area to see if she was

being watched and sat across from me. "So how've you been holding up?"

I held back a yawn and sat up straight to fight off my sudden urge to sleep.

"I took your advice on the motel, dirt cheap—"

"Or just plain dirt!" Her lighthearted giggles punctuated the interruption.

I couldn't help but let out a quiet chuckle. "Yeah, but thanks, it's home for now. Hopefully not too long."

Someone cleared their throat loudly from the back of the restaurant. I saw a portly man wearing an apron standing at the back of the kitchen with his arms crossed. He had a stern look on his face, eyes locked on Melissa.

"Rats," she said, looking over at her manager and then back at me, rolling her eyes. She stood back up and got back to business. "What'll ya be eatin' tonight?"

I waited about ten minutes before Melissa brought my burger, hot and juicy. She was polite but skipped the small talk since her boss was clearly on her case tonight. I ate slowly, trying to enjoy every bite. I wouldn't be doing much eating out without a job. After I finished, Melissa came back and sat back down.

"So, I forgot to tell you." She paused, unsure how to phrase her next sentence. "After you left the other night, some guy was asking about ya."

I scratched my head, trying to think of anyone that would know me in town. I had a friend who moved over to San Francisco a while back, but we lost touch over the years and I hadn't even told him I was coming. And that was hours away. I racked my brain for a few more seconds until I got that sick feeling in my stomach. I thought back to the man that kept looking over at me at the diner and then the generous tipper who knew my name.

"Who was he? What did he say?"

"Well, he didn't give me his name. He was wearing a dusty old suit, had a bushy beard and greying hair, but he looked forty or so. Know him?"

Sometimes paranoia can be a blessing. I've tried to fight the feeling of being watched my entire life, but more times than not, I've found it to come in handy.

"I can't say. I'm straight off the bus, remember? What did he ask you?"

"He asked me if I knew you and how often you came here. That was it. He had a funny way of talkin'. Real deep gritty voice, like if a lizard could talk. Kept clearin' his throat too."

I shook my head in denial. Who would be looking for me? "Did you tell him anything?"

"No!" Her reaction seemed to surprise her. She looked to see if her manager noticed and continued in a whisper. "No, and he definitely didn't give me a cop vibe, and kinda gave me the willies." She paused again. "*And* I don't even know your name, sugar." She batted her eyes mischievously, her eyelashes fluttering.

I shot her a curious glance. "As long as I can trust you," I smirked. "The name's Hagaki."

"So *Hagaki*, who do you think he was?" She asked with genuine curiosity.

"I honestly couldn't tell you. You're the only person I've talked to here for more than a minute."

"You probably just reminded him of someone. Or just chalk it up as another weirdo in this town. You'll get used to it." As she laughed again, I couldn't help but hear the southern twang to it.

"There's been a lot of weird stuff happening in the past few days though."

She shot me a semi annoyed look like she had already heard it all. "Yeah? Like what?"

"Well, the past two nights, someone's been calling my room at 4 in the morning."

Melissa rolled her eyes playfully. "Come on, those rooms go through so many owners, shady ones too. Probably just someone looking for their dealer."

I wasn't deterred by her explanation. "And today someone dropped this in my hat while I was playing in the street." I pulled out the oversized faded paper. "And they called me by name!" My heart started beating faster as the energy in me grew.

She eagerly leaned in and scanned the document, her eyes widening with excitement. "Okay, okay, that *is* weird. It says it's from 1888. This looks pretty rare too, probably worth some green."

I took the paper back and looked it over. In my rush after the unknown tipper, I hadn't taken the time to take in what I was holding. From the text alone, it appeared to be an old one hundred pound piece of currency from England. While I had never held one before, something about it felt so comfortable.

"So I'm not going crazy?" I asked.

"Oh, you already are for coming here with no place to stay lined up, but we're all crazies one way or another, right?" She grabbed a pen from her apron and scribbled something on a napkin and handed it to me. "I don't know much about this kinda thing, but it sure looks old and collectible. Here's the directions to a pawn that specializes in old history stuff. My ex used to be into that kinda thang. You can ask for Mort. I think he's the owner of the place."

I examined the napkin and my face lit up with a broad smile. "I'm so glad I met you."

"It's fate, hun." She stood up and smoothed out her apron. "See you soon, kay?"

I nodded and went for my wallet. She walked a few feet and turned back to face me. "Coffee's on the house." She gave a sly wink and headed back to the kitchen.

She sure knew how to earn a tip. Her advice alone had been worth every penny. Plus, she was acting as my personal concierge to this town. I looked at the napkin again. Grossman's Coin & Pawn. Maybe this Mort character might give me some info on my mystery donation. I could only hope.

I followed Melissa's directions down to a T but it still took me 20 minutes of searching to find the pawn shop. After passing what seemed like all the shops in the area, I finally saw the small sign in the window plainly labeled "Pawn". The shop was huddled in between a few office buildings on the far side of a dead end, a good block from any other retail stores. Inside, the store wasn't like any pawn store I'd been in before. The actual storefront was small, but from the outside, it appeared to be connected to the warehouse behind it. I scoped out the room to see it was filled with all sorts of artifacts and artwork. A thick layer of dust covered most of them, telling me they were just for show or were saved for the rare collector.

I walked further into the dimly lit room to find the typical pawn items; guitars, CD players, a few knives, nothing special. I got the impression that those were just there to offset all the strange-looking statues and paintings. The artwork didn't have too much of a theme other than they all looked dated, at least 100 years old or more. I saw Egyptian Statues next to clearly European influenced oil paintings. I got excited seeing some Chinese-style pottery like the kind I had made years ago.

I was lost in fascination staring at the items when the curtained wall rippled open and a short grey-haired man hobbled out. The Asian themed drapery blended so well with the décor that I hadn't noticed it was acting as a makeshift door. I tried my best to hide my surprise, but I sensed the old man got a kick out of it by the faint smile on his face. The swaying cloth behind him slowly settled back into place, giving me a chance to catch a few glances into an expansive dark room. He noticed my curiosity and cleared his throat loudly to get my attention. I walked up to the counter where he stood, shuffling around items on top of the glass display case.

"Hi there, Mort?" He nodded, ever so slightly. "I was told you deal with rare items?" I felt stupid immediately, considering I had a few minutes with all the rarities in the shop.

He smiled and spoke in a heavy Swedish accent. "Depends on what you consider rare, my friend."

I glanced around, my eyes drawn to the bright colors of the paintings on the walls. "You have a very impressive collection. Your place is pretty hard to find."

Mort wore a proud smirk, oozing with confidence. "Those who aren't willing to look don't deserve to find."

"I guess I really wanted to find it."

He nodded, motioning towards the note in my hands. "Is that what brings you here today?"

I realized I had been holding the old paper the whole

time and handed it to him. "I'm looking for some information on this."

He took the paper and looked it over a few times with a puzzled look. He pulled a small jeweler's loupe from under the counter and surveyed the paper.

"Where did you get this?" he asked, still inspecting the document.

"Someone gave it to me earlier today. As a tip."

With one eye still looking through the loupe, he adjusted the magnification with his free hand.

"Something is not right here. No, not right. Who gave you this?"

A chill ran up my arm and I felt my palms getting clammy. "I didn't see. I was busy playing my guitar."

He put down the magnification tool and set the paper in front of him. "This banknote is normally an extremely important, quite hard to find piece of British History." His tone sounded grim. I swallowed hard, bracing myself for his next words. "Someone has deliberately added," he paused for a moment, "something, deep within the fiber stitching. I've never seen anything like this before."

"What is it?"

"I'm not really certain. There's faint text and possibly symbols. The script looks as if it far predates this document, but what sort of sense would that make?" He shook his head aggressively. "No, no, no. No sense at all." He stopped and looked up at me. "I'd like to show this to a friend with your permission. He is a retired History Professor, taught at U.C.L.A. He works at the museum now. If anyone can shed some light on this, it's him."

I heard a voice in my head assuring me I was on the right track. "Sure, where should I take it?"

"I can take it there for you. Just leave it here with me."

I thought it over and decided that this was the fastest and only option I had right now. I had barely any money, no car, and didn't know the area. If I wanted to have someone else look at it, it might take days or even weeks. It helped that I only had possession of the tip for a few hours, which wasn't enough time for me to establish any sort of bond to it. For the time being, it was just a free piece of old paper someone gave me. If I had it for a day or two, I would have probably made plans with all the cash it could net me. But now, even more pressing, I needed to find out what was written inside it.

"Yes, yes, I will phone him shortly. Oh, and you know my name—"

"Jay Hagaki." I extended my hand. After studying my face for a few seconds, we shook.

"Interesting name, *Mr. Hagaki.*" He cast his eyes back to the document and the perplexed look reappeared. "We will figure this out. Come back in a few days, Mr. Hagaki. What is your number in case I need to reach you?"

"I'm staying at the Silverline Motel, room 14."

He nodded again and looked back down at the counter. I turned to walk out and glanced over my shoulder. He stood frozen, staring at the banknote in wonder—as if I had given him some alien artifact.

11

———————

It was nearing midnight when I returned to the motel. Wondering if the sleazy manager had actually contacted the phone company, I decided to ask before heading off to bed. The bell above the door clanked as always as I walked in. The manager sat slouched as usual, staring down at the glowing light under his desk.

Muffled voices softly echoed from underneath the reception area. The curiosity in me piqued. What was so enthralling that he couldn't pull himself away? Approaching slowly, I attempted to eavesdrop on his viewing.

"We can't stay here forever," a young woman said, with gloom in her voice.

"We need to find a real place soon," another woman responded in an aggressive tone.

"Well you're not the one whoring herself out there, day after—" The sound cutoff as the manager realized I had entered.

His hands fumbled to turn off the sound, his expression tense with suspicion. I got the impression this guy was hiding something. It didn't help that he hadn't been a real shining beacon of customer service, either.

"Whatcha watching, buddy?" I asked, my voice tinged with curiosity.

He looked up nervously. "Uh, just some soap operas, you know—Soap Network."

He was a terrible liar. I couldn't place a face or name, but I heard one of those voices in person within the last few days. And every time I even walked by, this sleazy sweat stain had his eyes glued to that TV under him. My curiosity was building. I made a mental note to find out what was so interesting. But first I had to get to the bottom of these mysterious calls.

"Ah, cool. Maybe I'll check it out. So, did you get a chance to call the phone company?"

He took a deep sigh of relief and wiped away the sweat from his forehead. He clearly welcomed the subject change.

"Oh no, I'm real sorry. I'll call them right now for you, just a moment."

He picked up the receiver and mashed his dirty finger on the keys. I wondered what kind of person has the phone company memorized and why he was suddenly so eager to please. This guy reeked of trouble. And he just plain old reeked.

He pressed a button on the phone and put the receiver on the desk. Hold music played for a minute on the speaker until someone answered. The manager, whose name I found out was Walter "Wally" Lawrence, gave Paul the phone rep his information and account number.

"Yeah, well-uh, I've had an ongoing issue with a half-dozen or so lines in my motel. Rooms 12 on up haven't had service in about a year."

The agent on the line spoke in a gentle, calming voice, "Well Mr. Lawrence, it appears our techs were able to restructure the additional lines you requested. They appear to be all active as we speak."

"I didn't request that! I told you guys I was still thinking it over!" He pounded a fist into the desk. "Who authorized this?" Wally's volume rose, becoming more animated as he spoke.

"It appears, yes, it was paid in full and authorized by you earlier this week. Mr. Lawrence, normally that kind of service takes a few weeks, but our techs finished in just a few hours. Looks like you lucked out."

Wally's anger died as fast as it came. "So you mean I don't have to pay for anything?"

"No sir. And we'd like to thank you for paying in advance up through the end of the year. Perhaps your assistant or business partner took care of it?"

Walt's smile couldn't be bigger. "Oh yes, yes, my assistant. Silly me!" Walt grinned back at me like I was one of his long-time friends. I shot him back a scowl to remind him of my original issue.

"Oh, thank you. And uhhh—I wanted to check in on one of the lines. Should be 14. We've been getting complaints about some late night calls."

"Just one moment, please. Ah yes, I see a few quick calls logged here throughout the day. Unfortunately, we aren't able to disclose any details on the calls unless they were threatening and we clear the release through the proper channels."

Wally looked satisfied with the answer and was about to speak. I, on the other hand, was not and decided I'd get involved.

"Hi Paul." I leaned onto the counter and tried to do my best Sam Spade. "We've got you on speakerphone right now. This is Detective Case Anderson. We've actually got a bit of a situation right now. We have ourselves a missing persons case and they were last seen staying in that room." I had never impersonated a cop before, but the ruse felt so natural.

"Well sir—" Paul said.

I wanted to beat him to the punch and cut him off. "Now, I know we normally have to get this cleared, paperwork, my boss and your boss, the whole deal. This is extremely time sensitive and, to be honest, we're trying to keep the media out since it's a high priority, if you get my drift. Every minute counts, Paul."

Beads of sweat dripped down Walt's face, the look of shock at me hijacking his conversation. A few seconds passed until Paul responded in a less calming tone than before, but he did a good job trying to cover it up. "Well detective, normally we can't disclose this, but if this could help someone—"

"It really could. You could save her life." I already had him, but the extra drama was fun.

He gave me the number and times they called. He also volunteered that the number had never been called before I had arrived. I grabbed a pen off the counter and scribbled the information on a pad of paper. I thanked Paul and hung up the phone.

After the phone call was over, Wally looked up at me, confused and nervous.

"Was that all true? You're, you're a cop?" his voice wavered.

I rolled my eyes at him. "Just needed some information."

Walt's shoulders sagged and a long, satisfied sigh escaped his lips. I got the impression he thought he was off the hook. He grew shadier by the minute. I walked away and noticed he had immediately resumed watching the television under his desk. In the bright glow, his obsession shined, smiling from ear to ear like he was reunited with an old friend.

Taking advantage of the distraction, I stopped in front of the lobby door and I let out a loud fake yawn. I extended my arms over my head and felt around the top molding to find my fingers were inches away from the greeting bell. Propping myself up on my toes for a moment, I silently pulled it down, palmed in my hand. That sleaze was hiding something, and I was going to find out what.

12

———

I left the office and looked around the parking lot for a vantage point where I could keep an eye on Wally. I found a phone booth on the other side about forty feet away. A rare occurrence today, but it was still 2007 when smartphones were just starting to get popular. Before everyone and their grandma had their own smartphones, before six-year-olds were charging up insane phone bills by accidentally buying everything with a bright flashing screen. I kind of miss the time when I wasn't tethered to the rest of the world, but not having a cell phone these days brands you a Luddite.

As I stepped closer to the booth, the hum of the electric transformer filled my ears. It was empty—and nonfunctioning by the mess of wires hanging from where the receiver should have been. The glass was covered with graffiti tags, which helped provide enough cover for me to see the office without making it obvious I was on a stakeout. I doubted anyone would even notice me, but if they did, it probably wouldn't matter. The area looked like a ghost town tonight. Even though it was nearing 1 in the morning, I figured the nightlife would be out on a Saturday. I leaned on the back of the booth and hoped I wouldn't have to be there very long.

It was strange spying on Wally. And a bit hypocritical. Voyeurism wasn't really my cup of tea and it didn't help that my subject was a shameless blob that hardly moved. Even from a distance, I could make out his head hanging low, aimed at the light that glowed under his desk.

It was times like these when I wished I still smoked. Not that I had the craving, but it was much easier to pretend you weren't stalking someone or just loitering when you had a cigarette in your hand. Not to mention it was one of the best ways to meet people, but I had left that habit long ago with my life in China. The chemical infused garbage they try to pass off as real tobacco these days makes me want to vomit.

After about fifteen minutes of fighting the urge to give up due to the creeping urine smell in the booth, Wally stood up from his perch and waddled his way over to the restroom. I leapt out of the booth and sprinted toward the office. The door opened fairly quietly now that I had removed the bell above it.

The stench of garbage hit me as soon as I walked closer to the back of the office. Candy bar wrappers, half drank bottles of cola, and empty pizza boxes found themselves hiding in various areas of the stained carpet. Wally was a real class act, but my mother taught me not to judge. My Polish one, but I'm sure my Japanese one would tell me the same as well. I've been letting them down a bit, come to think of it.

I scoured the area and found the source of Wally's amazement. A small monitor sat underneath the counter where Wally sat. It was tilted at an angle, which allowed him to sit back or put his head down and stare like I saw him do so many times before. Wasting no time, I turned the monitor on.

My eyes grew wide as I fought the sick feeling in my stomach. The bright black-and-white monitor buzzed a static filled screen displaying the inside of a motel room similar to mine. The monitor slowly blinked into focus. Two women. The camera was at a strange angle, pointed from a corner of the room towards the bed. One woman was lying on the bed above the covers reading a book while another was in front of the dresser, fixing her hair. In her underwear. The reality of what I was seeing sunk in.

I clenched my jaw hard, trying to fight the rage building up within me. The next channel on the monitor showed an older couple dancing slowly in the middle of the room. I heard a slow love ballad playing quietly from the screen's tiny speakers. The pig wasn't only watching, but listening in on everyone, too.

I kept flipping through the channels, knowing what I'd find. I kept telling myself maybe I wouldn't, maybe this was all just some weird prank or even a fucked up TV station. People aren't this horrible, I told myself. The third channel showed a single young woman putting makeup on close to her mirror. Her room was a complete mess, clothes and bags scattered all over. She turned around, now facing the camera. It was the girl from the bus, Olivia. A strange excitement swept over me as I saw her face. She grabbed a purse off the messy bed and walked out of the camera's view.

I leaned back from the screen and looked out the office window to see her locking her motel room. My gut reaction was to leave and go to her, but I quickly remembered I had the pervert to deal with first. Continuing my search, I changed the channel to see a view of another room, empty. My guitar sat in the corner. I closed my eyes for a second and took a deep breath. I had more than the proof I needed. There was no other explanation for what I was seeing, even though it had been painfully obvious from the start.

The restroom door opened with a jarring squeak. Wally shuffled his feet towards the office, humming a happy tune to himself as he got closer. My eyes burned with fire and my body felt like what I imagine a car does when it redlines.

He walked in and stopped at the door with his jaw dropped. "Wha, what are you doing bac—" Not giving him a chance to finish, I launched a closed fist into his nose.

He screamed in pain as we both fell backward onto the cold cement ground. I rose to my feet quickly and dragged him back into the office. He was easily over three hundred pounds, but I managed to muscle him in front of the monitor. I had let the anger take over, and I didn't want to stop it. He tried to talk, but the blood from his nose dripped onto his lips, causing him to cough.

"You pervert!" I screamed directly in his face while grabbing a handful of his greasy, thinning hair.

"I-I didn't do—" Walt coughed loudly several times

and struggled to talk. "I didn't do it! I swear. They...paid me..let me watch." His eyes looked glazed over while I kept my hold on him. "They installed it."

I leaned closer, directly in his ear. "WHO!" My grip still tight, I forced him further toward the counter.

He squirmed frantically, but it was no use under the pressure of my full weight. "He just put them in, I don't know!"

I wasn't sure if I believed him or not. Wally seemed like a sick, sleazy guy, but this type of setup seemed a bit more high tech than something he'd be able to pull off alone.

With one last motion, I grabbed the back of his head and threw it against the monitor. His head bounced off it, leaving a small blood smear on the screen as he fell limp in front of it. I was hoping to get some answers from him, but he was weaker than I imagined. Or I underestimated myself.

I stood up and looked down at the mess on the ground. Walt was still alive, but I had completely knocked him out. A part of me enjoyed the satisfaction I saw from the bloodied voyeur laid out on the ground. Another part was worried that I had lost control and caused it all to happen.

On my way back to room 14, my mind felt bogged down with so many questions. Who would pay for such an expensive phone repair without the manager's knowledge? I wondered if the same person that paid for the phones was the same one calling late at night. The timing seemed too coincidental.

And it was all happening at a motel with more bugs

than an embassy. If Wally was to be believed, he didn't know who paid for the equipment. Not that I believed him, though. The cameras seemed the work of a sick, sick voyeur. Just thinking about the monitor made me uneasy.

I made my way up to the room, thinking about the strange document I had received earlier. More questions came to mind that I tried to justify as realistically as possible. I tried to keep myself from panicking. Telling myself that everything going on could have a logical explanation. Except the mysterious tipper knew my name. How did I get into this mess? I laid down on the bed and closed my eyes. Just for a moment.

PRETTY MUCH FAMOUS

The gunshot jolted me awake. I opened my eyes to feel a sharp pain in my brain. A flash of the view from my seat in the greyhound bus bound for California. Blinking through the pain, my vision returned with a newfound focus. I propped myself against the headboard, covered in sweat, heart racing like I had just gone out for a sprint. Looking around the quiet, dark room, I realized the noise came from within my mind. But it wasn't just a dream. It was too vivid, too real. Another memory unlocked, but this was different. This wasn't a previous body's experience like my time in China. It was from another timeline.

All the strange things happening to me started to make sense. I had already lived through this part of my life before, but the first time, everything was different. Sort of. Like I told you earlier, I was famous once. I just hadn't realized it until this fear riddled moment. That fame got to me, though. To the point where I would do anything just to be "normal" again. I guess I found a way out. A way back to the life you've been reading about for the past ten thousand plus words.

You see, when I stepped off the bus to California, the first time, I never went to the diner and met Melissa. I slugged my guitar over to the first coffee shop I saw and, to my luck, it was open mic night. I ended up being a regular there. For about three years. I worked various odd jobs like giving private music lessons, working as a car wash attendant, and playing some local venues. Until one day, I was discovered at that very same coffee house. My rise to fame was fast.

The future that was

I was Jay Hagaki. Chart topping rapper, slowly transitioning into a rock artist. At the time, most of my fans didn't seem to mind the new direction I was taking. But all the record executives warned me it was a bad move. I had made them eat their words after they saw my latest album's sales. The Blu-Ray for my bio-pic released soon after and that sold fairly well despite my distaste for it. I didn't think I could act, but everyone thought otherwise. To be fair, I was playing myself. Regardless, I'd made a deal for two more movies—which I was not looking forward to.

A couple million fans, I was known worldwide. Now I wasn't an icon in the game just yet, but I had been touring for two years now and made my way up to being a household name. My third and final album, the rock one, had critics saying I had solidified myself as a true artist since it had made me more versatile. All it meant to me was that another tour was about to start and I really wanted a break.

I had money, millions. The record sales gave me a solid paycheck, but I racked in the real cash from the last two tours. Along with that, I put my name on a clothing line at Kohl's and had a brand of vodka ready to debut. The clothing line I was okay with, the latter, not so much.

Funny thing about that, I didn't even drink. One of the clichéd stereotypes I had avoided was being the alcoholic or drugged up Hollywood wild man. I don't want you to think I was Mr. Wholesome either, that isn't the case. Even though I looked 28, I had already made and learned from my mistakes living out my life as a Japanese farmer in ancient China.

Seeing that I remembered my life in the East, it shaped a lot of who I had become. At the time, I never understood how I had such detailed memories, but often my experiences would help me make the best decision. I often felt like I had a leg up on everyone else. It made me rich, successful, and a pretty decent role model, despite some of my lyrics. I was an all-around stand-up guy in the media's eyes. To the outside world, I had it all. On the inside, I had emptiness.

I don't want to make it out like being famous was the worst thing in the world, because it had lots of advantages. I was able to do some great things for a lot of people. But it turned into a nightmare after a few years. All my years of experience and now I found myself dancing like a marionette to my label—which is pretty common these days, I hear.

The same music that got me noticed by the label was now unacceptable and they chose to take it in another direction. My first two albums only had one song written by me on each. They brought in some never-was rapper that called himself a lyricist and "worked with me" on the tracks. They paid him off, so the writing credits went to me, naturally. Would you believe I made all of my beats, too? Well, according to the album's credits, I did. The truth was that I was a pretty good producer, but my stuff was too "raw" for the mainstream consumer. So again they brought in a man touting himself as a beat-smith and reworked everything I made.

Early on, I took it for what it was. I was getting help from the industry's best. But over time I started hating taking credit for work that wasn't my own. They billed me as a one-man band, a wonder kid, or *man* later on. In addition, I couldn't come to terms with all the changes they had made to me as both an artist and a person. I became jaded, angrier, more introverted. And they had successfully extinguished the creative fire within me.

I know that this isn't the most uncommon story with celebrity, but it's just the tip of the iceberg here. One of the breaking points was when they wanted me to commit a "low level felony crime to appeal to a harder audience". Their words, not mine. In addition, my label had actually sued me for releasing the rock album since it was against the image they built for me. I had paid for its production out of pocket. Once they saw the sales, they dropped the suit and kept the whole ordeal a secret. It was supposed to be the equivalent standing atop a mountain with my middle fingers pointed high screaming "Fuck You". It was my last attempt to bring back some of the creative flair that made me feel alive. But in the end, all they saw was dollar signs. And it brought me down even further.

I had only myself to blame. I had stupidly fallen into contracts with the label. For all my years of experience, I was pretty naïve. More movies, more albums, more tours, more things with my name on them. I wanted to break from the contracts, but I was no good at the Hollywood game. I had made commitments, and I'm not the type of man to break a promise. Plus they had threatened the people around me if I walked.

For months after my third album, I juggled being on tour and making public appearances every day. The final straw came on the night of the Hagaki Vodka release party in Las Vegas.

13

Late 2014

They reminded me for weeks to be at the release party at precisely 9:00 pm. The clock read 8:45. I sat on my bed in the hotel room, ignoring the cell phone vibrating, dancing closer and closer to the edge of the nightstand. I didn't want to go anywhere tonight. Branding the Hagaki name was just another thing that made the executives see dollar signs. Being named one of 2014's Men of the Year last month made it even more alluring. Now I had to hock alcohol.

If I had to put my name on something, vodka was one of the last things I'd pick. It's not that I hated it, but it's led to some really strange experiences. It doesn't seem to affect me in the way others describe. I don't even feel a slight buzz. The last time I had a few drinks, I saw things, heard things. It's an unsettling feeling.

Either way, I wasn't keen on Hagaki Vodka. Despite being vocal against it, I ultimately lost and had no say in the matter. The idiots built an entire release party around something with my name on it against my will. Did they really expect me to show?

Banging erupted from outside my door before I could answer that thought. I didn't answer and laid back down on the bed.

"Hey!" My manager's muffled voice fought to make it through the door. "Open up Hagaki, we're late!"

The door buckled from the pounding until I finally responded. "I'm sick, go away."

I heard a few muffled voices outside the door. They weren't going to be that easy to get rid of. The doorknob started turning aggressively.

"You're coming with us no matter what!" the manager said, with more anger in his voice.

I heard more whispers from outside the door. The knob started turning again with even more force. I got off the bed and looked out the peephole to spot a man with a small device plugged into what I assumed was the door's key card reader. Next to him was one of my many managers, Julio, and his bodyguard.

I secured the chain and stood back. Even if they got in, they would need to force me out. A loud chime beeped outside the door, letting me know they had just cracked the key card code. Without wasting time, they opened the door and found the chain blocking them from opening it fully.

It became abnormally quiet for a few seconds until the loud pounding started. From the small opening in the door frame, I could see the bodyguard ramming his shoulder with full force. The door was sturdy, but the hulking guard was easily causing the door to cave in. On the fourth and final try, the chain snapped away from the wall and he tumbled forward into the room.

He tried to regain his balance after launching into the room, but I took advantage of my position in the bathroom and snuck up behind him. Using his forward motion, I immediately jammed my knee into his massive back, sending both of us to the ground. Still on top of him, I grabbed both of his wrists, snapping his arms towards his backside, all while pushing my knee even harder into the small of his back.

The brute screamed in pain as he wriggled around, trying to break free. He had a good eighty pounds on me and it showed as I started to lose control. He fought my grip on his wrist and got his arms halfway towards his sides. I shifted my grip and felt the muscles in his wrists tense under my touch as I hit pressure points.

As my fingers dug deeper, he squealed and soon went completely limp. He lay face down on the carpet of my room, his breathing slow and steady as he drifted off into a deep sleep. I let go of his hands while my body shook from the adrenaline coursing through me. I tried to stand, but felt the sharp sting of ice against the back of my neck.

WAKING UP WAS ABRUPT, smelling salts being shoved in my face. My head jerked back and my eyes shot open. I tried to ignore the throbbing in the back of my head and looked around to find I was in a limousine. Julio was sitting across from me with the bag of salts in his hand.

"Wakey wakey, you pain in my ass," Julio glared at me and extended his other hand, "Here. Take some ibuprofen for the head and get your ass out there. We'll be at the premiere in minutes."

Normally I wouldn't have trusted Julio, but right now, he wanted me alive and alert. I took two pills and washed them down with a bottle of water. I tried to shake off the cloudiness in my head. I sighed and laughed sadly, seeing the tight penguin costume I was shoved into.

Julio shook his head and responded snidely, "Everyone is going to be there. Be on your best behavior."

The lights outside the windows shined through brightly, even with the deep black tint. I heard a small crowd outside the door, most likely expecting my arrival. The car cruised to a halt and I could see a red carpet laid directly outside my door. I sat motionless.

"What if I just decide to sit here instead?" I coughed out.

Julio smiled eerily as ever and pulled a medium-sized pistol from his suit coat, pointing it at me.

"I swear to God Hagaki, nothing more I would love than to blow your fucking head off right here, right now. You get out right now and put a smile on." He lowered the gun to the floor. "And if you don't," he cackled, his finger hovering over the trigger, "then you'll take the blame."

I nodded my head in disgust, trying to hold back my rage. He watched carefully as I put my hand on the door, ready to open it. At the last moment, I launched my other arm out and slapped the gun away from him. Following with the same motion, I turned my body and punched him as hard as I could with my other hand, sending his head slamming back into his seat. I grabbed the gun from the floor and tucked it into my waistline as he sat sprawled out, unconscious.

Tonight had pushed my limits too far. Julio, while annoying, was just a pawn in making my life hell. I looked over to see him slumped over. Small drops of blood dripped onto the leather from his open jaw.

"Everyone's going to be there, huh?" I repeated to myself as I opened the door to a red carpet, complete with flashing cameras and cheering.

14

———

I stepped out onto the carpet and closed the door quickly behind me. After adjusting my tie, I stopped halfway down the aisle giving the photographers plenty of good picture opportunities. Being in the spotlight was a hard habit to break after a few years. After a few seconds of fake smiles, I snapped out of it and realized why I had actually come.

I continued towards the doors and realized I hadn't even paid attention to where the party was being held. I looked up at the marquee before I approached the doors. Of course, it was being held at a high-class gentlemen's club. Located on the side of one of the ritziest hotels in Vegas, Nyte Skye looked like the kinda place CEOs went to unwind after a day of corporate takeover and ruining lives. This event had Julio's mark all over it.

The doormen pulled open the double doors as I approached, sending a wave of loud electronic music pouring out. A beautiful thirty-something blond woman greeted me. Dressed conservatively in a black business suit with hair pulled up in a ponytail, her thin framed glasses screamed all business. The suit was tight, hugging her more than ample chest and thin frame. While she was almost completely covered, I caught a glimpse of her long, toned legs below the grey skirt. She seemed uncomfortable in the clothes, leading me to suspect suits weren't part of her normal wardrobe. She caught me looking and smiled.

"Good evening, Hagaki. Welcome to my little club." She had a valley girl quality to her voice that didn't match her business woman attitude. She nervously extended her hand. "I'm Amber," she said with a soft giggle.

I took her hand, and by the look on her face, surprised her by leaning closer to kiss it. She blushed and looked away for a second like she was trying to hide her excitement.

"I'm sorry," she batted her eyes, "I'm not normally like this. I'm- I'm a big fan!" Her bright smile beamed back at me with the kind of warmth that could melt most hearts. In fact, I'd bet that was a common occurrence. Unfortunately, or fortunately, depending on how you look at it, my few years of fame had hardened my heart.

I had become extra guarded against anyone new in my life. From my experience, they either wanted money or a chance at their own fame. Amber looked pretty well off money-wise, so maybe it was the latter. I wasn't a bad-looking guy, but I didn't think I was really a stud either. It's funny what fame does to you. The fine folks at People voted me into the top ten best looking of the year, go figure.

I figured I'd lighten up this time and smiled back at her. "Oh, I bet you say that to all the celebrities."

She shook her head and folded her arms, still beaming. "No, Honestly! I was so happy when your manager booked my place." She looked around to make sure nobody was close and leaned in. "I had your poster on my dorm room wall."

Amber stayed close, her eyes twinkling as she smiled into mine. I sensed her working up the courage to speak again when I heard a shout from across the club over the loud music.

"Gak! Gak over here!" We both turned to see Paul Jackson, an actor from my latest film, at the bar raising his glass.

"I guess I shouldn't hold you any longer," she said, with a hint of disappointment in her voice. "If you need *anything,*" she trailed off, her lips curving into a seductive grin.

I smiled and bowed, then headed over to the main area of the club. I stopped at the entryway and looked around to see it was filled with a lot of faces. I recognized most of them, about 40 or 50 in all—record executives, some actors from my film, a few members of the press and half a dozen musicians I'd worked with. I didn't see any booths in the club. Everyone was standing at the bar or near small tables scattered throughout the dimly lit room.

The club was smoky, not from cigarettes, but from fog machines positioned at various areas near the runway. Soft lights glowed throughout the building in warm, relaxing tones. Two scantily clad women were on stage dancing with each other provocatively, still clothed but I didn't expect that would last for long. Another woman danced atop a raised platform at the other end of the club, which had most of the room's attention by a count of all the turned heads.

I looked up to see a second level overlooking the first floor and stage. The stairs leading to the other level were gated off—as if the place needed any more exclusivity. Every footstep I took was a battle as I fought the queasiness in my stomach.

While I love women and have been to places like this in the past, I would have never picked a strip club to host this sort of party. And it's no secret how I feel about having my own line of vodka. The worst part about it was that it was all done without my knowledge. Once I finally found out, I had a front-row seat to sit back and watch. A naïve kid signed his name away. I know, I screwed up.

I took a deep breath and continued walking forward; shaking hands with a few of the people I called friends. The music got louder as I closed into the main area near the bar. I almost reached the counter when a bright light shined above me. I looked up to see a blinding spotlight pointed directly at me.

The music screeched to a halt and the DJ's voice boomed over the speakers. I stopped dead in my tracks after realizing I was technically the guest of honor.

"Ladies and gentlemen, the man of the hour, Mr. Jay Hagaki!"

The room burst into light, followed by a rumble of applause. I saw that even the dancers had stopped gyrating to clap with everyone else. A waitress approached and handed me a wireless microphone. I turned it on as the applause died down and the room settled around me.

My eyes scanned over the patrons in the club while I fumbled around for the right words to say. I had been threatening my label with retiring for the last three months and this seemed as good of a time as any. But for some reason, it didn't feel right. I had the classic dilemma of a devil on one shoulder and an angel on the other.

Ruin the label's plans and tell them I had no part in this or just flat out retire? Or take the high road and thank everyone for coming even though they just wanted their pictures at the big glamorous release party?

I took another deep breath and started, "Thank you all for coming out tonight. It really means a lot to me." A few people cheered. Some obviously had a bit too much to drink already. "Growing up as a small boy in Poland, I heard stories of my ancestors making their own vodka from the potatoes on their very own farm." I almost slipped and said Japan. That would have looked great.

A flowing black velvet curtain dropped from the other side of the room, uncovering a giant crystal 'H' with a few bottles of my branded vodka surrounding it on a pedestal. While it sounds pretty tacky, I have to admit the logo was sleek, and the display oozed elegance. I took that as my cue to walk over while continuing my speech. I wasn't too bad at improv, it seemed.

"They didn't just see it as something to change your mood or alter your mind. It was more about enjoying company, a little indulgence now and again. No, this vodka is not something made so you can drink to forget."

I picked up a bottle in my free hand and held it up high for display. "This vodka, you drink to remember."

The crowd cheered and clapped at my ad-lib speech as I continued. "Made from only the finest ingredients." I paused and looked at the bottle. It said "Made in Poland". The assholes at least got one thing right. "From my ancestors' farm in Poland, Hagaki Vodka!" The audience was still clapping as I set down the microphone and opened a bottle, pouring the first glass for myself. The next few seconds were a hazy blur.

The clear liquid fell over the ice in my glass, splashing the edges. The bottle was heavy in my hands, pouring until the cup was almost full. I raised my glass to the crowd with a smile, but behind the scenes, my mind filled with racing thoughts. A chill washed over me as I rapidly replayed the past few years in my head; the memories coming back in a rush. I wished so intensely that I could escape this life I had created. This fame I used for nothing. This prison of fake friends and over-priced material goods.

The crowd lifted their glasses towards me in unison, a sea of familiar and unknown faces. My head started pulsing with a burning sensation, like my brain was swelling and getting bigger than my skull. My extremities tingled, nerves dancing from a strange shooting numbness. I closed my eyes, only to see the dim lights from the club etched in the back of my head.

I raised the glass to my lips and took a sip in sync with the rest of the room. The cheers exploded, coinciding with the music that came back on full blast. I dropped my glass and spit out the awful liquid and stood there almost paralyzed with a foreign, indescribable emotion. Nobody noticed. The lights dimmed, and the room buzzed again with the energy of the crowd. I snuck back in the shadows. Free from fulfilling my duties, I let out a deep sigh of relief. The cold steel pressed into my back cut it short. I used my remaining energy to turn my neck and see Julio pressed in close.

"Fucker, the boss wants to talk to you." His lip had already swollen from the punch I gave him earlier and it looked like a black eye was forming. He pushed the gun harder into my back. "Move!"

The sensation slowly returned to my legs, making the walk forward a bit easier. Julio grabbed me and guided me up the second floor into the VIP section. My feet felt like they were sloshing through wet concrete, but I finally made it up the stairs. Julio corralled me into an office with tinted windows and slammed the door shut behind us.

I saw Terrance Stewart, Vice President of my record label and biggest thorn in my side, standing on the other side of the room. Dressed in his thousand dollar tuxedo, he had a sick grin across his face. He was in his late forties but didn't look it. Even in his expensive power suit, his greying hair and wrinkled face made him appear much older. He stood there watching us, casual as can be. Julio backed away to give us some space, his gun still pointed at my back.

The burning swept over me again. First in waves until it swirled over my entire body, this time even more intense. My legs went completely numb, yet I stood without issue. I kept reliving the same thoughts like a broken record. Everything about this night was wrong. The past few years felt wrong. Inside my mind, a tornado was spinning, gaining momentum with no signs of stopping. It was feeding off the rage and emotion building within the small room.

Terrance slithered closer to me with the same sinister smile. "Tonight is going to be our night, Hagaki." He put his gloved hand on my shoulder and patted me like a child. "You've been good money to all of us, Hagaki. You've made a rich man even richer and for that I thank you immensely."

His words echoed over and over in my head, bouncing off my brain like a drum. Dizziness swept over me, but I kept my balance while he continued to talk.

"But alas, you've become such a pain to deal with." He backed away and grabbed a small black case from his coat. "So now it's time for your contract to expire. The good news is that I have all the rights to your estate, so you can still keep me rich beyond the grave. So kind of you." He opened the case and pulled out a syringe with a reddish liquid.

I tried to speak, but nothing came out. I wasn't even able to move my mouth to mime it. Stuck in place, my nervous system frozen. And the unease still grew within me. I was soaking up some supernatural force like a sponge and I was almost at max capacity.

"I've noticed you entertainers have a lifespan of about two, three years at most. Five if I'm really lucky. You remember your friend AJ, don't you? He was really good to us. Even better after his *mysterious* disappearance from the spotlight a few years back. I have a good feeling your record sales will skyrocket just like his."

I always wondered what happened to AJ. The rumors ranged from elaborate conspiracy theories to alien abduction. I guess it always boils down to greed. We had been in the middle of planning a track together when he disappeared. While I didn't get to know him too well, he seemed like one of the good guys.

Terrence started pacing the room slowly, talking in a mocking tone. "Hagaki, Oh I loved him dearly, like a son. And you know, I think he looked up to me like a father. It's a shame he declined bodyguard protection. I just keep thinking what if—what if he had protection during that mugging after the event?" he stopped and laughed. "Well, I'm still working on it. I have a few hours to get the wording right."

The numbness started spreading throughout my entire body now and was competing with the rage. The whirlwind in my brain started causing an excruciating pain shooting through my spine. Time slowed while I watched Terrance nod at Julio. This was it, my execution. Murder to make me a martyr. Just to sell even more records.

Behind us, glass shattered and the lights flickered. A soft feminine voice. For a split second, my body freed from the invisible shackles. In a complete blur, I pulled the gun from my waistline and sent my arm upwards. A bright light filled the room as a loud gunshot seared my eardrums. The lights dimmed as the blast echoed for what felt like an eternity. Warm liquid ran down my face until there was only darkness.

Darkness. And then my life flashed before my eyes, backwards. Like I had pressed rewind on a VHS tape at the speed of a week per second. The events flickered in my brain so vividly, so clearly, so fast. And then it stopped.

Until it began again with my reflection in the dirty bus window.

15

───────

So there I was back in 2007, alive and living a good seven years before that night. A second chance. While I remembered most of that alternate timeline now, there were a few gaps that were still slow to fill in. Reflecting back, when I first found myself on the bus, I felt odd but didn't know why.

When I set foot in San Diego, things felt strange, yet familiar. I initially brushed it aside, trying to convince myself I was just being paranoid or suffering fatigue from the long trip. But now, after waking from the dream, or whatever that was, I knew it couldn't have been a coincidence that I was being pulled forward into a strange series of events.

A new sense of disappointment washed over me. I had once hated what happened after being in the spotlight and now with my do-over, I unwittingly followed a path back to stardom. Was time itself trying to course correct, arranging each new interaction? I wondered, even with the same goal of being famous, I had taken a different path the second time around, met different people, made different choices. I feared what the consequences might be—I've seen the movies. You can't mess with time.

Back to what was in front of me, I remembered I had received the number of my mysterious caller from the phone operator. I grabbed the phone cord and plugged it back into the wall. Then it hit me. It seemed far-fetched, but was someone calling to interrupt my dreams? Trying to prevent me from remembering? If Wally was to be believed, there was someone else watching these rooms. I wondered if they were waiting until I entered REM to break my cycle. Setting aside my paranoia, I looked down at the crumpled piece of paper.

I dialed the number, the sound of the dial tone ringing in my ears. The line rang three times before a series of short clicking noises and then silence.

A robotic female voice responded, "Enter code now."

I froze while trying to think of anything I may have seen that could have been a code. My eyes shot around the room in a poor attempt to trigger a thought, but came up with nothing. After a few more seconds the line clicked again and I heard the dial tone. I scratched my head and sat on the bed wondering what it all meant.

I tossed and turned in my dirty motel bed for hours while the thoughts raced through my head. My heart was pounding as if I had drank a pot of coffee and had to stay still. I tried to clear my head but the thoughts kept returning. Sweat dripped from my forehead, getting into my eyes. I ran my fingers through my long hair—tugging at each strand like I was trying to pull out the thoughts.

My breathing became labored, everything blurred. I spiraled downward in a chasm of irrational thoughts mixed in with justified paranoia. It felt as if someone was sitting on my chest, trying to crush my ribcage and I was powerless to fight back.

Out of nowhere, I found the energy to spring out of bed and tear off my clothes as I rushed into the bathroom. I turned the shower knob to release a stream of icy rain all over my body. I shivered under the cold water for a few minutes, turning the water off when I lost feeling in my toes and ankles.

I grabbed a towel and wrapped it around myself, still shivering with my teeth chattering. While my body was thawing back to its ideal temperature, my brain was at a standstill. I'd curbed my thought process at the cost of freezing my body. With my remaining energy, I walked over to the bed and collapsed on it, still sopping wet.

I had fallen asleep for about twenty minutes when the phone rang. I raised my head from my sprawled out position on the bed and looked over to the clock. The soft red glow said it was 3:00 am. Half dazed, I crawled toward the phone and blindly swiped in the noise's direction with all my strength, almost falling off the bed myself. I launched the receiver several feet away until it bounced back against the nightstand and hung still after being pulled back by the cord.

Satisfied, I set my head back down on the pillow hoping to go back to sleep. As I settled in, a voice came from the dangling receiver.

"Hello? Hello?" The muffled voice sounded frantic. I rolled over and tried to ignore it hoping it would go away until I recognized the voice. "Mr. Hagaki? Are you there?" Mort raised his voice as loud as I imagined the small man could.

I rolled back in the other direction and grabbed the phone. I cleared my throat before I answered. "Mort, that you?"

There was a distinct sense of relief in his voice. "Thank heavens, I thought they'd gotten to you already! Listen—"

"Wait," I cut him off, still sleepy. "What... *Who* are you talking about?"

"We're still piecing out the details. We need your help with that, but I don't think you're safe right now."

I sighed, wondering what I had gotten myself into. "Did you find something on that paper?"

"Yes, Yes.. Hagaki, look out your window. Carefully. Is there anything unusual out there?"

"Uhm, hang on." I grumbled and put the receiver on the bed. The urgency of his tone still hadn't sunk in. I walked over to the window and peeked out from a small opening I made in the blinds. The parking lot was shady in its own right, so I wasn't sure how to answer Mort's question.

My eyes darted around the parking lot, still adjusting to the flickering street lights. The lot was still and looked extra desolate this time of night. With nothing amiss, I studied each car. Most were junkers, but one car stood out. A silver BMW gleamed in the moonlight, parked on the far side of the lot. I couldn't make out any details other than the engine was still running. Even though it was just a hunch, I had a sick feeling in the pit of my stomach. Someone was inside waiting for me.

I came back to the phone. "There's a car that doesn't belong. Looks like it should be in a showroom. Are you going to tell me what's going on?"

"In person. Come to where we first met as soon as you can. Make sure you aren't followed." The line went dead.

I hate when people are so cryptic. But I could only imagine he thought someone was listening in. I threw my clothes on in a hurry and was about to leave the room when I thought of the car parked outside. Peeking out the window, I saw it was still there. The metaphorical light bulb turned on over my head as I ran over to the phone and dialed the police.

It rang for a few seconds until the dispatcher answered. "9-1-1, what is your emergency?"

Never having made an emergency call, I imagined they would be frantic and awkward. "I - I'm at the Silver-line motel... and... uh... the owner got in a fight with some guy."

"Has anyone been injured sir?"

"Yeah, Yeah... the owner, he's knocked out cold... bleeding."

"OK sir, I'm sending an ambulance now. Did you see who did this?"

"He took off... I, yeah... I think he's still in the parking lot. Silver car."

"OK sir, if you're staying at the motel, please stay in your room. We're sending officers now."

In a few minutes I'd have the distraction I needed. Plus Walt had this coming to him anyway. Two birds.

"That man, I heard them fighting... he said the owner had hidden cameras in the rooms, he said he saw the TV under the counter."

"Sir?"

I dropped the ruse. "Tell the police to check the equipment under the counter."

I hung up and waited until I heard an ambulance in the background. Soon followed by a police siren blazing, I knew this would be my best chance. Red and blue lights filled the lot as I opened the door just enough for me to creep out.

As I crawled through the darkness to the end of the second floor, I saw the ambulance pull up to the office. I continued crawling along the balcony until it wrapped around to the other side of the building. The entire parking lot was now filled with lights and radio chatter from the ambulance and police car. Now out of view, I took the alternate staircase down and sprinted far away from the motel.

I ended up sinking into a good pace which I kept the entire time on the way to the pawn shop. Being a few miles away, it took me a little over thirty minutes to run there. Maybe the car belonged to some rich visitor and I had overreacted—but it couldn't hurt to be extra cautious with how frantic Mort sounded on the phone. I cut between a few buildings and alleyways, confident I wasn't being followed.

As the clock ticked closer to 5 am, the sun emerged from the gritty steel horizon. The city was asleep, no signs of activity outside the store. I turned the handle to find it opened without a struggle. Inside, there was no trace of Mort or anyone else.

"Hello?" echoed to no response.

I continued looking around until I saw a piece of paper taped near the makeshift curtain wall.

Hagaki,
Please meet us at Dr. Hannigan's office.
We believe the banknote indeed has a message in it, directed
at you.
We need your help to decipher it and fear it is a warning.
I apologize for all the secrecy but I will explain it all in person.
Mortimer

UNDERNEATH HE LEFT the address to the doctor's office at the history museum. I was getting sick of this wild goose chase. Just as I was about to grab the door handle to leave, I caught a glimpse of a silver BMW creeping down the street.

16

I ducked to the ground, out of view from the window. From the floor, I reached my hand up to lock the front door. The blinds were part way closed giving me some cover, but I decided it was best if I crouched and made my way to the warehouse entrance.

Before leaving, I pocketed the note in case the stranger found their way in and dug around. I continued crawling through the makeshift fabric door that led into the warehouse. The dim lighting made it difficult to see through the maze. In the darkness, I inched closer to a light in the distance. With the room now illuminated, around me stood giant crates and boxes with what I assumed were statues and artifacts. I eyed an exit next to the manager's office at the far end of the warehouse.

Before I exited, I noticed a brown trench coat and fedora hanging from the rack by the door. I threw them on hoping it might help throw off whoever was looking for me. From the style, I could tell it was Mort's. Luckily, it was oversized and looked somewhat normal on me.

I opened the back exit and peered around the corner. The street was empty. A loud knocking echoed from the front door of the shop. I estimated one, maybe two minutes until I had more guests. Not taking any chances, I headed out into the alleyway.

I soon found myself two blocks away from the pawn shop due to my quick pace. A block in front of me, a city bus slowed as it approached its next stop. At that point I didn't care where it headed, as long as it got me further from whoever was following me. I ran full speed toward it, catching the doors just before the driver was about to close them.

I startled the old man, causing his hands to tremble on the wheel. "Wooah, didn't see you there!" He held the door open long enough for me to hop up the stairs.

I threw change in the meter and sat near the front. "Thanks," I said, a bit out of breath.

I finally allowed myself to relax after being on the run for the past hour. After a few minutes, I turned to face the transit map behind me. The bus headed out of the way I needed to go, but it connected to another route running directly back to the history museum.

By the time I reached the museum, the sun had risen and its rays were warming the street. Without delay, I ran up the stairs to the entrance and pulled at the doors to find them locked. I realized the note said they would be in his office, which I assumed would be close. Across the street, I noticed a small two story building housing the offices.

I ran to the other side of the street and tried the main entrance. Another locked door. Just as I was about to curse my luck, I saw the faded sign. *"Please buzz for entry after midnight."* I held my finger on the buzzer for a few seconds and stood back in the doorway. After a few minutes of waiting, Mort came down the lobby staircase and opened the door for me.

"Come in, come in," he said with urgency. "We were getting worried. Did you make it okay?"

I followed him into the building as the door shut behind us.

"That car I told you about.."

"Yes?"

"I distracted the driver and got away from the motel, but they followed me to your shop."

"Oh dear. Did they—" he stopped nervously to look out the windows of the dim hallway, "follow you here?"

I grinned, shaking my head then gesturing at my outfit. "I took these and snuck out the back."

"Oh my, I didn't even notice you were wearing my clothes!" His laughter faded away to a look of disappointment. "You're stretching them out!"

He was right. They were uncomfortable and snug. In fact, I think I heard ripping at some point on the way over, but at the time they had served their purpose. I laughed and followed him up the stairs into a brightly lit office.

He introduced me to his friend, Dr. Erich Hannigan, and filled him in on the details of my night. Hannigan had a look of concern on his face adding to the wrinkles. He looked to be in his late seventies and carried himself well from what I could tell.

While Mort recalled my escape, I looked around the

office to see a few expensive looking tools scattered over a workbench. On the bench sat two large magnifiers, several small trays of liquid, and what I guessed was a special type of imaging light. I wasn't sure what kind of work the doctor did, but I got the impression he was familiar with art restoration.

"I don't want to be rude," I said in a less than pleasant tone, "but could you please tell me what the hell is going on? Who is chasing me?"

"Hagaki." Hannigan said my name with a slight Irish accent. "This document. Do you have any idea why you were given this?"

I shrugged. "No, I was hoping you could help give me some idea on that."

Hannigan flashed a gentle smile and nodded. "As you may have gathered, this is a one hundred pound banknote, printed by the Bank of England in 1888. These are hard to come by these days, as this denomination was less common and most have been destroyed. Typically these were held by high end businessmen and criminals, and could be exchanged for silver at one point."

"Erich!" Mort interrupted. "Just tell him what it says already!"

"Very well," Hannigan conceded. He walked over to the workbench and picked up the paper with a pair of rubber tipped pliers. He then placed the document under one of his magnification machines. "While this document is an uncommon piece, I have studied one in my younger days. Lights, please." He motioned to Mort, then picked up the imaging light. After turning a knob, he pressed a button on its base.

It emitted a high-pitched hum that rattled my ears for a moment. The doctor made a joke about it warming up. Mort found it funny, but I was in such deep suspense I didn't acknowledge it. I leaned in for a closer look. The device reminded me of a black light you'd find at a novelty store, except its casing was steel and had rows of buttons and switches all over it.

After Mort switched the room's light off, the soft green glow of the doctor's device filled the space. As the light grew brighter, he flipped a switch on the magnifier, which I realized doubled as a projector. I turned around to see the document quadrupled in size, clearly projected directly on the wall.

"Now when I originally saw the document, I noticed the colors were all distorted," said Mort. "I used my magnifier and found strange etchings inside various locations around the document, which is why I immediately sought Dr. Hannigan."

The doctor nodded in agreement. "A wise decision." He laughed and picked up a laser pointer with his free hand. "As Mortimer mentioned, you can see these areas here." He clicked on his laser pointer and circled a few areas on the wall. "Clearly these have characters that should not be there."

I leaned forward and looked at the areas he mentioned. I wasn't too sure what I was looking at, but deep in the paper's fibers I spotted some symbols. Realizing I was squinting and leaning forward, I relaxed my gaze and stepped back.

"Now, I can tell you're not familiar with this at all," Hannigan said, "So I'll leave the fun science and chemical testing out of it. That someone has altered the document in such a manner, with the same inks as originally used, is quite remarkable."

He stopped and turned to Mort. They gave each other a solemn, knowing glance.

"The symbols you see here are surprisingly common throughout history," Mort interjected. "Several secret societies' insignia, occult imagery. Alone, these would be nothing special. But seeing them together in one document, it's unheard of. It's like someone went out of their way to do this." He stopped, deep in thought.

"To get our attention," the doctor concluded. Hannigan then pointed the green light towards the document, which showed up on the projected image. "Now with this setting, the device is set to mimic direct natural ultraviolet sunlight on the paper fiber."

I looked even closer to see that the document had taken a new form. The strange symbols turned into eerie red ancient characters.

I leaned in closer and translated out loud. "Traveler." I stopped and took a deep breath. I had no doubts now. "They are looking... for... you." My Ancient Chinese was a bit rusty.

"Yes!" Hannigan clapped his hands together with enthusiasm and became more animated. "We have been able to piece some words together but I am not fluent in this dialect. My colleague who specializes in Chinese history was only able to make out a few words, but they sounded like—"

"Shut up and let him finish, Erich!" Mort lashed back.

"It's hundreds of years old," I said with confidence.

I studied the glowing words in awe. It was so long since I saw this style of writing. Whoever wrote this knew me well—or at least some of my past.

"You are in grave danger." While familiar, I had to focus intently on each letter to decipher it. "Find her and keep moving. I will find you when you are not being watched. Stay away from shadows." I paused after finishing the message. "Wow…"

"There's more," Hannigan said. "Look here." He pointed the laser at a small section next to the message.

I walked closer to the image at an angle, trying not to block the light. "It's—I think it's a signature." I studied harder on the strange characters melded together. "I think it says… No, I can't quite make it out."

I lied. I could read everything. Along with the warning to lie low, there were several mentions of things I didn't quite understand. These men had helped me too much and I had a feeling the more they knew, the worse off they'd be.

We studied the document together, finding no other information. The three of us stood in silence, trying to digest the strange message. I ran my fingers through my hair until I noticed Mort staring at me with wide eyes and his jaw dropped.

17

I froze in position, my arm raised, hand touching my head.

Their expressions of shock and wonder had me concerned. "Wh-What?" I said.

Mort walked over to me and ran his finger down my triceps. "Erich, put your light on him."

The doctor walked next to Mort and repositioned the light. My eyes saw a flash of blue until he adjusted it lower to focus on my torso.

"Look, it's even brighter now! It's reacting to the UV cathode!" said Mort.

I craned my neck to see a vertical bar code running across the inside of my arm, starting from my armpit and ending at the elbow. It had a brownish-red hue to it like the text on the document but was much clearer.

Erich leaned in closer. "I've heard of these kinds of tattoos. Where did you get this Hagaki?"

It's one thing to learn something new about yourself

or even remember an old memory thought long forgotten. It's something much different to find out the body that you're stomping around in has a secret message on it. While I guess it can be argued that they're similar, you don't look at the inside of your mind day in and day out —at least not literally.

Needless to say, but I will anyways, I was dumbfounded. "I—" My brain was searching through its file cabinets, wardrobes, and Rolodex, turning up with no results. I was at a complete loss. My life has had its share of strange events and I was getting into something bigger than I could imagine.

I stood there staring at the bar code with a childlike curiosity. But hidden inside was primal fear. Fear that someone had branded me without my knowledge. Fear that my body was altered against my will.

"What the hell does this mean?" Paranoia built within me.

"Oh, my." Mort ran his fingers over his wrinkled forehead. "He's never seen this before, Erich!"

The shock made it hard to piece together a sentence. "How-how can someone have this kind of mark and not know?"

Hannigan invaded my personal space and stuck his face into my armpit. Good thing I showered. "Have you had any surgeries lately? Thought loss? Any time you can't account for?"

I didn't know how to answer his question honestly. The past few days were one long blur. And time loss? My life was a series of dissociative moments and trying to return to reality. I shook my head and shrugged, hoping that he'd have some other suggestions.

"Well, it has to mean something," Mort pondered as he started to pace the small room.

"Barcodes are so commonplace," said Erich, thinking out loud. "We use bar codes for the museum's entire inventory. And for shipping, tracking, hell my employee badge has one that lets me into restricted areas."

"It must have a purpose, Hagaki. We just need a way to find out how to read it."

The two men stood there thinking until I interrupted them. "Can't we just go scan it somewhere?" I said. They were so caught up in their theories that they hadn't thought of the obvious.

Hannigan's eyes lit up as he started to smile. "You're right! So simple. The shipping area is closed, but we can try scanning you at the museum's gift shop!"

The three of us walked down the stairs and across the street to the museum. I was nervous at first; worried my friend in the silver car would be waiting for me as soon as I stepped outside. I looked through the sleepy streets—it was nowhere to be seen. It was an hour before the museum opened, so Hannigan let us in through a side door. After entering his code on the electronic keypad, the door unlocked and we hurried into the building.

Hannigan led us through the basement corridors, passing through the steam tunnels under the museum until we reached the service elevator that took us to the main floor. There were several employees walking about and preparing the exhibits. Hannigan smiled and waved with confidence, allowing us to pass through without raising any questions. The gift shop was near the front of the building and looked like it would be ready for business as soon as the museum opened.

The doctor explained our situation to the hapless store clerk who stood behind the counter scratching her head. After several minutes of trying to explain it to her, he pulled out a smaller version of the imaging tool and again lit my arm. This allowed the UV ray to illuminate the bar code once again, helped by the fluorescent lights in the room.

I showed my arm to the young cashier. "Scan me." She looked dumbfounded but decided to play along and grabbed the scanner.

She focused it on the code and pressed the trigger. After a few seconds she turned to the doctor, "Nothing."

"Hmmm," Mort put his hand on his chin. "Ah, of course! Your system is only looking for items in its inventory." He walked to the other end of the counter and took a look at the register.

"Ah, see young lady," he acted as if he was teaching her a lesson. "There is a Universal Mode here. Several code types as well. Let's try them all."

Hannigan remained still as he held the light on me while Mort kept trying different modes, scanning me over and over. It was one of the most awkward sights to see. The cashier was trying to fight back laughter until she couldn't hold it and giggled. She walked away laughing, leaving us alone in the gift shop. After several tries, I heard a beep come from the register.

"Ah-ha!" Mort pointed his index finger to the air while beaming a smile. "We have—something."

The three of us walked around to the register and looked at the screen. On the display was a series of 14 numbers that didn't mean anything to me. I studied the screen to see if maybe it might reveal something else. Just the numbers.

"Maybe it means nothing?" said Hannigan.

"Well, it has to mean something!" Mort ran his fingers over his chin.

I wrote down the number while they went back and forth—figuring it may come in handy. They started getting louder with their outlandish theories, to the point of bickering. I got the impression that they butt heads often. The cashier came back to the counter from her laughing spell and shot the men an annoyed look. Mort got the hint. We walked out together into the museum's lobby.

They continued their conversation while I distanced myself from them. I needed some space to think. I needed to find out who was trying to contact me.

I leaned against the wall, focusing on my breathing. The relative silence was short lived as the museum began to open for the day. The overhead system kicked on with a jazzy eighties new wave song. The beat was so familiar, where had I heard it before?

AJ! He had sampled the beat in his first big hit. Throughout all the madness, I forgot about my colleague from the future. I realized I could save his life if I reached him in time, but that wouldn't be so easy. This was a different world than the one I once knew. Just a few days ago, at least in my mind, I was a rich celebrity with every-thing at my fingertips. Now I was back at the beginning with no money and a new goal. Instead of aiming for fame, I was trying to figure out who was following me. And maybe I could stop a murder in the process.

Pacing around the lobby, more thoughts raced through my mind. While helpful, I didn't want to drag Erich or Mort any further into this before I knew the extent of what I was dealing with. They were nice enough to get me this far, but I didn't need anyone else to worry about.

Looking at the number in my hand, I kept trying to think of what it could mean. I was sure it was the answer to my questions, but I didn't know how to make any sense of it. I slipped the paper into my pocket and felt the previous note from the motel. I pulled out the crumpled piece of paper and stared at the phone number. It was a long shot, but I decided to give it another call.

I interrupted the discussion with urgency in my voice. "Is there a phone around here I can use?" I asked.

Hannigan looked around, frightened for a moment as my interruption tore him out of the deep debate. He pointed to the information desk about thirty feet behind me and went back to a look of strained concentration as he tried to remember what thought he left off on.

The man at the reception desk had no problem with me using their phone since he had seen me enter with the doctor earlier. I dialed the number I'd scribbled down from the phone company operator and waited for the prompt.

"Enter code," the robotic voice buzzed. It seemed less human and more computerized this time. I took my time entering the code, pressing each button with intention. I took a deep breath and pressed the last digit. Silence. I was locked in suspense until I heard a quiet clicking sound. It lasted for about ten seconds until the robotic voice returned.

"Welcome back, Traveler." I almost dropped the phone. Stunned, I regained my composure and listened to the voice list off a series of prompts. Once again my world started to spin. The mixed emotions of shock, confusion, and fear began to build within me.

The prompts seemed to have no end. "If you wish to request a vehicle, press star twelve."

My head was shaking in disbelief. "No, no, this doesn't make sense," I said in a hushed tone.

"I'm sorry," the voice chirped back, "I don't understand that command."

I dropped the phone letting it swing to my side. It hadn't even mentioned voice prompts. I tried to act as calm as possible, smiling at the receptionist who was now looking me over. He had a curious gaze, probably wondering why the color had drained from my face.

"Is everything okay, sir?" he asked, with an overly inquisitive tone.

I reached for the phone and returned it to the wall. "Oh yes, yes...I'm such a klutz, sorry!" I tried to laugh it off and did a horrible job. I told you I wasn't a very good actor. I started to back away when I noticed Mort and Erich looking in my direction with puzzled looks. I wondered if they had been watching me the whole time.

Paranoia started to sweep over me again. What could they be talking about over there? Maybe they thought I was an alien. Hell, if they knew my real story they'd probably want to run all sorts of tests on me. Realistically, I figured their next step would be to get more of their colleagues involved to see what they could come up with. I concluded that the more people involved, the worse I'd be in the long haul.

"I have to go to the men's room!" I picked up my pace and started for the exit on the other side of the museum. Using momentum to my advantage, I blasted the glass doors open. Fresh air filled my lungs as I jogged down the steps toward the street.

Not even halfway to the street, tires screeched as a silver BMW slammed to a halt fifty feet in front of me. Their parking job in the middle of the street gave me the feeling they were here for more than the new exhibit. Both doors opened and two men in grey suits emerged. They were clean shaven with short dark hair and dark sunglasses. They could have passed for secret service or other government agents, but their clothing was a few decades out of style. Not to mention covered in layers of dust. Other than the scar across the passenger's face, they looked identical.

A few seconds later than I should have, I realized they had come for me. No doubt they had traced the phone call. Their less than friendly entrance sent me running back into the museum. Maybe I could lose the twins in the steam tunnels we passed earlier to get in. My feet pounded hard on the rich marble floor as I hurried toward the service elevator. I looked behind me for a split second to see they were hot on my trail. Now in the employee area, I jumped in the old elevator and pulled the gate closed. I pressed the down button repeatedly, hoping to speed up the old steel contraption. A loud bell rang behind me as the gears started grinding away, beginning my descent.

The twins rushed into the room and stopped a few feet away, watching my slow escape. They glanced at each other for a moment and without communicating, one of them backtracked out of the room. The other rushed up to me and rammed the cage with his shoulder. The elevator shook violently then halted while I was knocked into the back of the car. The suit bounced backwards, losing his sunglasses in the process. I caught his bright blue eyes staring back at me. He winced and shielded his face with a hand, as if he had looked into the sun. His other hand felt around aimlessly for the sunglasses.

The grinding of the gears grew into a loud whining of steel against more rusty steel as the car began to inch downward again. The suit found his glasses and stood unfazed. Now only a few feet away, we met face to face with only the bars between us. The air in the room was frigid, as if it had dropped twenty degrees.

He broke the gaze and pushed his arm through the gate, clawing at me. I jumped back just out of his reach and huddled in the corner, wishing the elevator would move faster. After what seemed like an eternity, he backed away as I lowered further down. He stood and watched me slowly lower out of sight. The lack of emotion on his face was haunting. I tried to relax the rest of the way down but my heart felt like it was going to jump out of my chest. I pressed my back to the wall and practiced a minute of deep breathing. Calm ran through my body until the elevator slammed into the ground floor, bringing the adrenaline back.

I unlocked the gate and hoped I'd have enough time to escape before the other suit caught up to me. Before both feet hit the ground, a hand grabbed my wrist and pulled me forward.

18

––––––

"This way, now!" the deep voice commanded. They didn't give me a choice, tugging at my arm.

I looked up to see an older man, maybe in his fifties, with long grey hair and a full salt and pepper beard. He was equal to my height and had a similar build, but I could feel his strength far outmatched mine from his force.

He pulled me through a maze of corridors and guided me through the twists and turns. Familiar with the layout, there was no hesitation in which direction to go next. He realized I was now following him and let go of his grip. I followed close behind, keeping up with his lightning fast pace. I obeyed him, if only because I was already being chased and needed a way out.

We darted from tunnel to tunnel until it became clear we were not in an area that was used often. Most of the lights were out and old debris littered the murky ground. After a few minutes of splashing through the tunnels, we reached a steel gate blocking our path. Behind the bars lay more dark corridors with a hint of sunlight creeping in the distance. The man looked back for a moment and then reached into his black suede jacket. Either it was the adrenaline or my newfound trust; I stood unfazed as he pulled out a large handgun. He raised his hand and slammed the chrome against the rusty padlock. It exploded upon impact, sending reddish-brown pieces onto the cement. He leaned into the gate but it only moved an inch.

"Come on! This weighs a ton!" he said, fighting the steel with his bare hands.

I joined him and grabbed two of the bars, pressing my entire body weight into it. It turned forward as we pushed. Rust popped off the hinges, creating a new pile of brown residue under our feet. My biceps started burning but I kept pushing through the pain. My arms shook causing my grip to loosen. The sweat accumulating under my palms caused my grip to slip. I was losing energy fast, so I decided on one final push. I leaned in and pressed in as hard as I could. Not the best idea. My fingers slipped off the bars and the momentum sent me head first towards the gate. My shoulders crashed into the frame and my head poked through the bars. I regained my balance and realized in this position I could push with better leverage.

As I walked it forward, the gate creaked open until it hit the uneven cobblestone ground. It wouldn't budge anymore but there was enough space for one person to fit through at a time. Loud splashing through the shallow water echoed through the tunnel behind us.

"Go!" he said, still gripping the bars.

I wormed my way through the opening and waited on the other side.

"Keep moving!" His voice boomed through the rusty bars. "We'll meet soon. Go, don't stop moving, just run."

Without question, I turned and headed into the dim corridor toward the light. My feet splashed in the pools of water underneath as I got closer. I took a hard left to find the source of the light—a sewer grate above me. I climbed the ladder and pushed hard up into the grate. It didn't pop right up like in the movies. This thing was heavy. I lost my footing and slid a rung down the ladder but caught myself and tried again. Lifting it up hurt my already spent arms, but the adrenaline was hard at work helping to block the pain. The sewer grate slid over with the sound of grinding metal. I popped my head out of the manhole to find I was deep inside the botanical gardens next to the museum.

I slid the grate back over the manhole and looked at my surroundings. The area was so quiet it was unsettling; not even the buzz of a passing insect could be heard. From a distance, two groundskeepers milled about through the lush landscape. For as long as I lived in California, I never had visited this place. I would have to take a trip here when I wasn't running for my life. I noted several other museum buildings in the near distance, each surrounded by ornate landscaping and pathways.

A rough estimate of the sun's position told me it was 9 in the morning, explaining the emptiness. I kept a fast pace, trying not to raise attention to myself as I passed two groundskeepers. They continued with their day and kept talking as I passed. Once I was closer to the street, I sped up my pace, trying to put the museum behind me as fast as possible.

I had no idea where I was running right now, but the grey-haired man told me not to stop moving. Since he hadn't killed me and helped me escape, it would be foolish not to listen. Plus I had nowhere else to go. My motel room was being watched. The pawn shop was off limits now that they had tracked me there. I thought about going to Arthur's. Even if Melissa could help, we had just met and dragging her into this wasn't that appealing. I didn't want to add any more regrets if she was hurt on account of me. Mort and Hannigan seemed to mean well, but my paranoia warned me not to get them involved further. I tried to think of somewhere else to go, but every thought was a dead end.

I kept running until I came to a busy intersection. The number I called had options for all sorts of goodies that could help me now, but there was no doubt that the call triggered the suits. I ran past the intersection and continued my trek. I had fallen into a trance, repeating the man's words in my head. Nothing mattered now. I blocked out the world and lost myself, racing forward. The only thing on my mind now was moving. As abruptly as it had started, my body tore me back to reality.

Awake through the night and without proper hydration or nourishment, my body started to fail me. First, my legs. Heavier and heavier with each step I took. The pounding became jarring, sending shock waves up my spine and until it reached the base of my neck. Next came the burning from the pit of my stomach. It was pleading for energy but I had ignored it and headed onward.

My ignorance lasted half an hour. Soon my pace turned into more of a shuffle. Every muscle was telling me to stop. It was at this moment I realized that my body was still in the shape as when I had first arrived in California. I had let myself go a bit after becoming a celebrity —only focusing on keeping my weight down instead of building practical muscle. But now, back in my pre-fame days, I took better care of myself. Even though I had conditioned for speed, not distance, I lasted a while. I snapped out of memory lane and grounded myself to the present.

For the first time in hours, I stopped. I found a street vendor and bought some bananas and a bottle of water. I sat on a curb a few feet away and ate all three bananas and drained the water in a matter of minutes. The vendor had stopped what he was doing and watched with eyebrows raised. Whether it was fear or compassion, he handed me another water bottle and an apple.

He smiled warmly. "Free of charge, son."

I nodded and accepted the gift. I sat there for a few more minutes, letting my body go into recovery mode. My body ached. Muscles I hadn't used in years pulsated. But it felt so good to catch my breath. It was the equivalent of jumping into a hot shower after being stuck outside on a winter's night. Stopping was the right choice. After the fog in my brain settled, I rose to my feet.

My legs were unsteady. I knew I had a few good hours until the delayed muscle soreness kicked in. I nodded to the vendor and mumbled my appreciation. He must have deciphered my gibberish—he smiled back at me and nodded. Moments like that made me thankful that some people cared. He went the extra step to help a stranger. Even more to his credit, I probably looked like a crazed madman. Dirt mixed with the sweat on my face, my clothes reeking of the sewers.

I took my time walking the next few blocks until I came upon a bus stop and collapsed on the bench. Hopefully far enough that I had lost them, whoever they were. *"Keep moving!"* echoed in my head. Would taking the bus count as moving? I decided to take the chance. My body needed to rest. My aching legs wished I had stopped sooner.

The bus came a few minutes later. I could see the driver getting impatient at my slow walk up to the door. The bus was half empty. Or half full? Nine others sat scattered throughout, minding their own business. The driver slammed the door hard as soon as I stepped up. The door tapped my back, propelling me forward to almost trip up the stairs. I corrected my balance and walked up the steps to deposit my change. Even before I sat, the bus was back in motion.

Once again, I found myself leaning against the window of a bus. The sounds of the bus accelerating and breaking became melodic. The constant hum of the engine put me at peace. My eyes started to get heavy. I chose not to fight it.

My wake up call was much more pleasant this time. I opened my eyes and looked outside to see it was starting to get dark. The small clock in the front of the bus said it was almost 8 o'clock. I yawned and rubbed the sleep out of my eyes while the bus passed row after row of clubs and bars with bright neon signs. I watched the nightlife through my window for at least another hour.

To fight the fear creeping in, I told myself the running would soon be over. I was a marked target with nowhere to go. I couldn't live my life as a fugitive forever. Especially from the unknown. The bus grew smaller with every minute as the steel walls seemed to close in.

The bus pulled to a stop next to an Irish pub to let a few more passengers on. My eyes remained focused on someone outside the window. My heart skipped a few beats. Olivia was walking out of a bar right outside the bus. She looked around for a few seconds and leaned against the brick wall next to the bar entrance. She reached into her purse, searching frantically until she shook her head and went inside.

Just like when I first saw her, the same feeling swept over me. The bus doors slammed shut, breaking me out of the trance. *Find her and keep moving.* The words etched in the banknote flowed through my mind. This couldn't be a coincidence.

"Wait!" I said as I jumped out of my seat. "This is my stop!"

I tumbled toward the front as the bus came to an abrupt halt. The driver looked at me and scowled before opening the doors. The warm air hit my face as I set foot out the door. I turned in the bar's direction, the odd feeling still flowing through me. This felt right in some magical, unexplainable way. I walked through the pub doors and looked around for her.

OLIVIA

Some of what follows is a glimpse into her world, after the fact. I did my best to piece together her experiences using my own memories along with her notes.

~

A sharp ice pick seared through my skull.

Headaches came and went, but this one was different. Like something crawling inside my brain and then, just as quick as it started, the pain stopped. I shrugged it off the best I could and headed back into the bar.

I quit smoking a few months ago, but the cravings still hit out of nowhere. Lucky for me, my purse was cigarette free tonight. I don't know why I thought I'd have any, but I needed to get out of that bar to clear my head, even if for a second.

The women's bathroom reeked of cheap perfume and sewage backup. Dive bars weren't known for their rosy smells, were they? I looked into the mirror and checked my makeup. I decided to go with dark red eyeliner and mascara tonight. It didn't match the green and pink streaks in my dark black hair, but I didn't give two shits tonight. I just wanted to drink until the world didn't make sense, or maybe the other way around.

I checked myself one last time in the mirror and made sure I wasn't coming out of my dress. I wasn't really a dress girl, but it went along with the whole "trying new things" approach to life I was going for.

This whole vacation was my therapist's idea and so far it was making me more depressed. It sure beat living back at home, though. At least here I was depressed and confused instead of just depressed. My therapist thought it would clear my head and help me see the world a bit more. Her advice was to take chances I would have never taken back home in Salt Lake City. She told me to be more spontaneous, more outgoing, and to try to make life not a job. Easier said than done, I told her.

We came up with a list of do's and don'ts that were no brainers. She didn't want me getting knocked up or shooting up. Nothing illegal, nothing dangerous, blah blah. She should have realized when she told me to live life, I'm going to do it on my own terms.

A group of obnoxious younger girls walked in the women's room chatting up a storm and broke my introspective vibe. I took that as my cue and walked out of the bathroom. I was getting annoyed with this place and decided I'd just tab out and head back to the motel.

And then I saw him. He looked just like the guy from the bus, sitting alone by the bar. He looked uncomfortable, shifting around in his seat and constantly scanning the room. My body did that thing where it feels you're falling fast for a split second on a roller coaster. I took a deep breath and swallowed hard. Something about him drove me wild. Not in a sexual sense, although he was cute—but on a much deeper level. When I first saw him, it was like I'd known him for years. I know people say that all the time, and I'm one of those people, but this was different. I saw something in his eyes that made me feel so happy and protected that it was hard to walk away from him when I did.

With all the new chances I've been taking, I should have at least left more than my silly note. But I had been too focused on not scaring him off. Was it that hard to leave my MySpace profile?

If it was him, I'd at least have to get his number this time. I left my cellphone at home, but I could always use the motel line. "Enough stalling Liv," I said to myself.

I walked toward the bar, pausing with each step. I needed to get a closer look and make sure it was really him. He, or at least the idea of him, filled me with a strange blend of excitement and fear. You're not getting obsessed again. Stop it. Even at the motel, I thought I saw him check in. But the chances of staying at the same place were slim. And I didn't think he was the type of guy to stay in a horrible place like that. Hell, I only picked it because it was the complete opposite of my first choice.

Now just a few feet away from the bar counter, I had a perfect view of his side profile. It was definitely him. I knew his face well from the vivid dreams haunting me late at night. I've had strange dreams before, but this was something new. Instead of having the same dream over and over, this one continued over the last few nights. My personal soap opera playing out in my head and I remembered the details.

My mind was trying to tell me something, and if by pure luck or coincidence, I had my chance to find out.

19

———

"Is this seat taken?" a female voice asked over my shoulder.

I turned my head to see her. Relief washed over my body. My mind wasn't playing tricks on me after all. She flashed an awkward smile as I hesitated to answer. I finally responded after realizing I had been lost in thought, ironically, looking for her.

"It's yours," I said, with my own gentle smile.

She sat on the stool next to me and smoothed the ruffles out of her shiny red dress. She looked uncomfortable in the dress, but it looked amazing on her. It hugged her curves just enough to leave something to my imagination and was classy, yet seductive at the same time.

"Fancy meeting you here," I said with a smirk on my face. "You look amazing, by the way."

"You aren't stalking me, are you?" She raised one eyebrow and smirked, but there was a hint of uncertainty in her voice.

"Well, to be honest, I was riding the bus and saw you

outside. I don't really know anyone in town and thought it'd be nice to see a familiar face, even if we've only talked a few minutes."

"I can appreciate your honesty." She motioned for another drink to the bartender and looked back at me. "What have you been up to?"

I wanted to tell her that my mind and body were exhausted from running all day long. I wanted to tell her I needed help, but I had no idea what kind of help I even needed. Going against the grey-haired man's wishes, I needed a moment to process what was going on. If I didn't give myself time to breathe and stop running, I would fall apart even faster.

"Still getting settled in. Been real busy lately though. This was my first chance to relax all day." Technically, I wasn't lying. The bus wasn't too peaceful. She didn't need to know the details. "How about you?"

"I originally came here to stay a week or two. But I've decided I'm going to look for work. It's only been a few days so I'm trying not to get discouraged."

"I think I remember you telling me you were pretty well off?" I asked.

"I am, sort of. It's complicated. I guess to answer your question though, yeah. I have money. But I didn't come here just for fun. I was hoping the change of scenery would help me get out of my funk. Maybe start over, stay a while, get my own place."

"A new place can be scary too, but there's a sense of adventure in an unknown place." I could lecture about that topic all day so I cut myself off. "What kind of work are you looking into? Acting, modeling?" Even through the makeup, I saw her cheeks turn pink. She looked away to hide her face. It was adorable.

She must have spotted my grin and shot back a sultry glance. I got the sense she was used to being in control and I had caught her off guard. She responded in a playful yet powerful tone. "Are you hitting on me, stranger?"

"Name's Hagaki, remember?" I had hoped she remembered my name, but our encounter was so brief. I tried not to let my disappointment show by exaggerating my pouty lips.

She landed a soft punch on my shoulder. "I'm just messing with you!"

I cupped my shoulder and massaged it gently, pretending it hurt. We exchanged a few anxious glances while taking in the music, until she broke our silence.

"Listen, this is going to sound kind of weird, so I don't want you to creep out." She appeared to be struggling to find the right words and looked nervous. "But seeing you has to be a sign or something."

"What do you mean?" I tried to hide the fact I had been thinking the same thing.

"I've been having dreams ever since we met," she trailed off and ran a finger around her wine glass to trace a circle. "Dreams about you."

I was listening before, but now I could barely hear the other sounds in the room over her voice. Normally I would have made a crude joke showing off my huge ego or saying how irresistible I am, but I was all business. I kept feeling something so different about her. The last time I remembered this feeling was when I met Lijuan, centuries ago. There was an aura around Olivia that kept drawing me in. I waited for her to continue so that I could hang off her every word, but realized she was waiting for me to reply.

"Dreams?"

OLIVIA, AGAIN

I regained my balance and tried to play it off, but I could see the concern on his face. His mood had already shifted in seriousness when I told him he had been showing up in my dreams. He took me as a guy that joked around a lot, so it surprised me he didn't make a crass joke and assume it was sexual. Instead, he listened intently.

His seriousness caught me off guard. I wanted to tell him to get it off my chest, hoping that would make the dreams stop. My plan of writing it off as a joke was ruined now that the tone of the conversation completely flipped and he was waiting for me to continue.

They took place over several nights, so I had pieced them together as best I could. Some of the minor details were a little hazy, but the dreams were vivid and seemed too real. The first night, I woke up covered in sweat, fumbling in the darkness until I realized I had been dreaming. The next two nights went a little easier, but were still jarring, to say the least.

I tried to get out of telling him, but he kept insisting on hearing it. A little embarrassed, I continued. My dumbass brought it up, after all.

It took place at least five years in the future. I was still in California, working in Hollywood as a dancer. An exotic dancer, but it was at a high class establishment. I'm not sure how I felt about that, but at least I wasn't a strung-out bottom of the barrel stripper. I was working the opening night of an extravagant party at the club. All sorts of people from Hollywood were there, including actors and musicians that seemed popular at the time. They weren't names I recognized in real life, except for his.

I was dancing on a raised platform near the bar when I saw him walk in. He was alone but seemed pretty important since the crowd went silent during his entrance. Someone handed him a microphone and he gave a speech that had the crowd cheering. I had even stopped dancing and clapped for him.

After that, it got a little fuzzy. I remember finding myself backstage in the break room. Another girl was covering for me while I sat back and drank some water. My boss, a prim and proper-dressed southern lady named Melissa, barged in and started yelling at me. She went into a rant, screaming about how I had no time to relax when such a high-profile event was taking place. She finished scolding me and sent me to the VIP area to make sure the guests were comfortable.

As I walked up the stairs, I heard a loud bang from the 2nd floor office. I had to have been close because my ears were ringing, even in the dream. Through the ringing noises, it sounded like there may have been a few more loud bangs but my hearing was fading in and out. Doing the opposite of most sane people, I ran straight for it and tore the door open.

After taking a sip of my drink, I closed my eyes and took a deep breath. I glanced over at him to see him nod for me to continue. He remained silent the entire time, hanging off every word. I took another deep breath and continued.

I described how I saw him laying, bleeding from the chest. His hand pushed against the wound, too weak to stop the blood seeping out. Behind him was the body of a shorter man, still clutching his gun. Sprawled out across the carpet, the short man had bled out from his neck. There was no question he was dead.

I rushed to Hagaki and helped press down on the wound. I was no doctor, but it looked like it was just shy of his heart by an inch or two. He was still breathing but his eyes looked glazed over, ready to fall into a deep sleep. I remember thinking that nobody had heard the gunshots, so screaming wouldn't help. I ran to the other end of the room and pulled the fire alarm. The screeching alarm replaced the music downstairs. I ran to the balcony and tried to get someone's attention. The club was in disarray from the alarm, but the DJ saw me flailing my arms. I looked back to see Hagaki trying to get himself up using one arm. I told him to sit down and wait for the ambulance, but he wouldn't listen. I didn't understand until I heard coughing from the other side of the room. A well-dressed man in a black tuxedo started clawing from behind a desk, struggling to pull himself up.

Now on his feet, I saw the white tuxedo stained with red splashes. While I stood frozen in shock, the tuxedoed man hobbled towards me with a strange look in his eyes. He limped closer, gaining speed, surprising for his condition.

And then I woke up, my heart beating a million miles a minute. It had felt so real and at the time, I remembered every little detail. It started fading soon after, so I had written what I could remember in my journal. Something told me it would be important, but I always write everything in that thing. I tried going back to sleep with no luck, so I decided to explore the nightlife and try to forget about it. It turned into hours of wandering around, lost in thought, trying to figure out what its meaning was—if any. The next two nights, the dream continued and took me for even stranger twists.

20

I tried to hide my shock. It seemed impossible. Her dream fit mine like a matching puzzle piece. There were too many details that were so specific it ruled out coincidence. Somehow, she had been involved in the life I had before I came back. Unless she had read my thoughts, it meant she was with me that night.

I had to know what happened after that night. My mind spun with possibilities. What else did she know? By the way she talked about me in the dream, it sounded possible that I might have survived the attack. The idea of living out an alternate future sent a shiver through my spine. It was the ultimate "What If" scenario, and I had a front-row seat.

"Your dreams are quite...vivid!" I poorly hid my mixed emotions and played it off as interest. "So, uh, what happened next?"

She looked up at me and studied my face. She tilted her head and searched into my eyes. It made me hope that my mind reading theory was wrong.

"Am I creeping you out?" She paused and took a sip of wine. I searched for words but came up empty. "Cause you have the weirdest look on your face right now."

"No, you're not. I'm just fascinated. Please, continue."

"Oh forget it." She looked away and played with her hair. "This whole thing is embarrassing!"

"Whatever, you had a dream about a stranger...and now you're telling him. What's the worst that could happen? I already told you I think it's interesting." Her expression was hard to read. "Please, I'm fascinated with dreams. They're kind of a hobby of mine," I lied. Personally, I hated dreaming. All I seem to have is nightmares. I felt bad playing dumb, but I needed to know what happened.

She looked back at me with a somber look on her face. "In the second dream, I took you to the hospital. I visited you every day for God knows how long until you recovered. The doctors all said it was a miracle that you not only survived, but still had all your functions."

Finally, good news. I'm not sure why it mattered, but relief swept over me. Even though it was a weird alternate future, knowing that I survived still had quite an impact. I smiled for a second and then reapplied my stone face of concern.

"Phew! What happened to the other guys in that shootout?"

"I think one of them died. I'm not sure about the other one. The forensic teams pieced the scene together and determined you were defending yourself."

Another deep sigh of relief. "And after that?" So far so good. At least in the future, I had some positives. I know

I'm a broken record here, but it's strange knowing that you, or at least a version of you, may be living out another life in a different reality. However, I would assume that the future-me is now the current me, since future-me wouldn't exist if I traveled. Wait—I think that's wrong. Isn't time travel supposed to happen to the troubled, smart people?

I came back from my trance to see her cheeks turn pink before continuing. "Okay, don't get the wrong idea here, it was just a dream..." I nodded with a faint smile, waiting for her to finish. "We'd been seeing each other for a while..."

"You mean we?" I narrowed my eyes and acted like I didn't understand.

"Yeah. Me and you, stupid! Yeah, I know, you were an uber celebrity, and I was just a dancer." She rolled her eyes, then softened her expression with a cute smile. "But we started going out. It was the first time I woke up smiling for once." She sat soaking in the moment as her face lit up with more joy.

Even before she told me, I had already figured that out. The feelings were so familiar, yet so foreign. My mind had been fighting what I felt for her, using reason and logic to tell me I couldn't have emotions for something I didn't experience. True, to my knowledge, I had only known her for a few hours on a bus ride, but I was feeling more than just lust at first sight. And I had plenty of experience with that in my past.

I returned a genuine teeth flashing smile despite trying to hold back. "I'm glad I made you smile, some version of me at least."

We shared another awkward but happy silence, until her smile faded and she looked away again. Her cute, nervous joy turned into concern and doubt. I got the impression these dreams had been screwing with her head. Maybe even as much as my unexplained feelings for her messed with mine.

"What's wrong?" I asked. She wasn't telling everything and I needed to know what.

"The most recent dream," she stopped and looked off into the distance. "Last night. It was a nightmare."

I saw sadness flicker in her eyes. One moment I had given her the giggles, the next she was already mourning over my grave.

"Hey, it's just a dream, okay? It's really interesting though, I'm listening." Part of me didn't want to hear it, but the curiosity won.

"Well..." She was fighting her urge to finish. My inquiring blue eyes stayed locked on her. I was pulling out the big guns for this.

"A few months later we—"

Behind us, a deep voice interrupted the conversation. "Hagaki."

We both turned to see the man who helped me earlier. His hair was in a long white ponytail and he wore glasses with a light green tint to them. He studied us before continuing. "Excuse us miss, but we must be leaving now." His voice was warm and friendly, despite the sharp command.

Olivia squinted her eyes before scratching her head. "Oh, uhm, okay."

"I need to talk to her, just a few more minutes," I said

with desperation. The man inched closer and closer behind me until cold breath tickled my neck. I was deciding what expletive to use when I felt a sharp pinch on my shoulder. A strange shiver flowed through my veins.

"I told you to keep moving, didn't I?" He grabbed my hand and twisted, exposing my forearm. I looked down to see the barcode with a murky red glow. "Dammit! They're still on to you. We're moving, now!" He kept his control on my hand and pulled me from the barstool. Now on my feet, I realized I had underestimated his strength.

Olivia fidgeted in her seat and bit her lower lip. She studied his face for a moment before turning away to finish her wine in one big gulp.

"We need to meet. Soon!" I said, while being pulled further away.

In the chaos, I looked back to see her mouth a number while waving a key. Though scuffed from years of abuse, the keyring's faded Starline motel logo confirmed where she was staying.

I nodded and turned to face my hasty friend. "Okay! You can let go, I'm coming!"

We sprinted out the door until we reached a shiny black sports car parked illegally in front of the bar. He extended his arm out to the car and pressed a button on the key fob. It responded by lighting the interior and unlocking the doors. I sank into the deep bucket seat, better suited for Nascar than a joyride. The man waved the fob in front of the ignition and it purred to life with a deep rumble.

Tires squealed and a wisp of burnt rubber crossed my

nose as he peeled out of the parking space onto the main roads. I couldn't see the display, but we must have been going at least 15 mph over the limit. The car danced in between cars to avoid any red lights, only hitting one which he blew through without regard. First the dizziness crept in. The world spun in a haze of lights. Next was the nausea. I closed my eyes to block out the blur, but I could still see the white lines flickering on my eyelids. And it didn't stop the heat coursing through my body.

I had so many questions ready to ask, but staying coherent was my top priority. I opened an eye to see him scanning the mirrors as he weaved between lanes until taking a sharp turn that had me clenching the arm rest. I imagined the car speeding to a secret Batcave-like hideout. Why wasn't I blindfolded?

The stuntman continued driving while I practiced my breathing, trying to regain composure. I was still disoriented after being ripped from Olivia. Poor Olivia. I wondered what she was thinking now. First, she has those dreams about me which most likely were remnants of another life. Then I'm whisked away with no explanation. And by the look on her face, she had recognized the old man, now sitting next to me in the driver's seat. Another wave of nausea swept over me, making it hard to concentrate. I wished for the ride to be over.

As if he was reading my mind, the man looked over and reached his hand near my neck. "I'm sorry." The dizziness came back tenfold. I felt so tired. Just needed to close my eyes, just for a minute.

I woke up groggy and in the same position. I searched my surroundings, only to find dark walls visible in the dim light. The smell of lavender and motor oil confused my senses. The man apologized again and bit his lip to hold back laughter.

"We're here. You can get out now," he said with calm reassurance.

Still pressing my hand against my head, I shot him a dirty look. "Where? And what the hell was that for?"

He chuckled. "A meeting place. And you didn't fall asleep fast enough." His smile turned into a huge grin. "I said sorry!"

After we got out of the car, he pressed a button on his keyring that opened the small garage door behind us. More doors and concrete walls. Instead of painted lines on the ground to divide cars, each section had a private carport. The fluorescent lighting and musty air gave me the impression we were several levels underground. The artwork and candles attached to the walls oozed opulence. Not to mention cameras everywhere. Whoever parked their cars here must be paranoid or rich. Or both.

"What the hell is this?" I asked, looking around while I walked out with caution.

"You've never seen a parking garage?"

"Not like this," I turned back to him. "Who are you?"

He motioned for me to follow him and cleared his throat. "You don't remember me at all, do you?"

"Of course. You led me through the sewers hours ago." I rolled my eyes.

He shook his head in annoyance. "Smart ass."

We walked up to a heavy steel door with E4 painted on it in big, bold print. He pulled out a keycard and waved it at the door. The invisible reader responded with a soft click, unlocking it. I followed him up several flights of stairs, trying to remember if I had ever met this man before today.

I couldn't figure out if or where I had seen him before. "No, I can't say that I do. Am I supposed to?"

"No, I suppose not. But it would have made things so much easier."

After a few flights, we stopped in front of another door. He pulled out the keycard again and pushed the door open, spilling light into the dark stairwell. The aroma of flowers punched my senses as we emerged into a vast lobby. Plush burgundy carpet cradled my feet as we walked through the lush landscape surrounded by trees. Flowers hung from the ceiling above, underneath the skylights with their view of the stars. In the center, a large marble fountain was busy at work pumping deep blue water through creatures of Greek mythology. Now closer to the reception area, I noticed a familiar woman standing behind the counter.

"Good evening Mr. Quinton," the receptionist said, with an unnatural happiness in her tone. The accent gave her away. I was looking at Amber from my release party. But of course the Amber here was seven years younger. I'd bet she'd love to hear how well she ages.

"Evening Monica. The usual, please."

Of course, she wasn't going by Amber yet. Probably her stage name. She turned to me and there was a moment of silence; her gaze intense and focused. "And your guest, Mister..."

"Hagaki," I said with a soft nod while extending a

hand. She didn't respond and stood motionless. I got the impression I had broken an unsaid rule.

Quinton looked at me and spoke as if I hadn't said anything. "He won't be staying the night. Thank you though." She handed him a small key card.

We were about to start walking towards the elevators when Monica looked at me again. "Pardon my intrusiveness sir, but have you stayed with us in the past? You look very familiar."

My stomach dropped as if I was in a plane and the seatbelt light was on.

"I—no. I'm sorry. Maybe I have a twin?" I smirked.

"Oh. I apologize. I must be mistaken. Enjoy your stay!"

I turned to Quinton to see him looking back with a slight grin.

"God, what a mess." He shook his head and we continued to the elevators.

"You still haven't told me what's going on," I said, keeping my voice low. The last thing I needed was Monica questioning us.

He tapped his key card against the elevator console to open the doors.

"It's clear you know what you've done." He entered the elevator car alone, leaving me staring back at him.

"I've followed you this far. Even after you knocked me out," I said in a rushed whisper, still trying to keep my volume low. "Why should I go any further? Why shouldn't I just knock you out now and leave?"

Truthfully, I knew why. Just how I felt something special about Olivia, I felt a unique respect for the man. I trusted him with my life, but I didn't understand why. Other than I had little choice.

"Because you want answers." He held out his hand to stop the doors from closing. "And by that quiver in your voice, because you know you wouldn't attack."

I paused for a few seconds and followed him in. He was right. His finger pushed the button for the fourteenth floor. We stood in silence as the elevator ascended. In less time than it takes to run my fingers through my hair, we had reached the destination and the doors sprang open.

"Come, we're almost there. You'll be safe soon," said Quinton.

More hints of an English accent I hadn't picked up before. Maybe he was hiding it. I followed, holding back my questions. He had the information I was looking for and I had a feeling he'd tell me soon. We walked down a long hallway, passing either hotel or apartment rooms on both sides. After what seemed like minutes of a boring, nondescript hallway, we came to the end of the corridor. A single door marked "Maintenance" faced us from the dead end.

He pulled a metallic key card from the inside of his coat pocket and inserted it into the reader. After beeping in a five or six-digit code, a loud click echoed behind us. I made a snide comment about the hoops we were jumping through as I followed him back to the closest suite. He ignored my comment and turned the handle to room 1479. Instead of finding the inside of a hotel room, another elevator waited for us.

He smiled and motioned for me to continue while he

locked the door behind us. I entered the elevator and noticed the console only had one button. Cute.

He joined me in the elevator and paused with his finger just in front of the button.

"One more thing. Don't let them scan you."

21

———

The elevator ride lasted much longer than the previous one. My ears popped a few times on the way up. I swallowed hard to get my hearing, only to have it fade away again. After a few minutes, the elevator slowed with a gentle halt and the doors sprang open. We walked out to a large office area filled with glass lined rooms. Only a few of them appeared to have personal items in them. The rest of the rooms were empty and collected dust. The overheads had a soft blue glow, making the light gentle on my eyes.

As we walked through the floor, I looked out the dark tinted windows to see we were in one of the tallest buildings in the skyline. Quinton led me through the maze of white collar boredom, stopping in front of two large doors.

"Before we go in, you must know that I was only instructed to find you and bring you here," said Quinton.

He stopped, trying to read my puzzled expression. I

took that as his way of saying that he would have answered my questions earlier if he could, but whoever gave the orders to find me said otherwise. Time to meet them, I guess. I grabbed the silver door handle and pulled one door open.

The heavy door opened easier than I expected. Inside, I found a dark conference room. A small wooden table big enough to seat about six sat in the center, flanked by walls dressed in designs from the 1970s. An older middle-eastern man, who I guessed to be in his seventies, sat at the head of the table with a younger woman to his left. They were both dressed in elegant, dark blue business attire. Both stood to greet me with a slight bow before the older man gestured for me to sit. I sat opposite them as Quinton found a seat next to me.

"We finally meet. Allow me to introduce myself," the old man said. "I go by Pharaoh, and this is my associate, Alycia. We've had our eye on you for some time now."

"A pleasure to meet you," I said with a hint of sarcasm. My patience had worn thin. I'd jumped through so many hoops tonight that I stopped caring what these strangers thought. "Now, with that out of the way, why am I here?" I asked with a sharpness in my tone.

Pharaoh chuckled before it turned into a soft cough. "I see Quinton was true to his word."

"I told him nothing, sir."

Pharaoh nodded and turned to me. "I apologize for this location. We don't use it often, but in a case like this, we needed to take every precaution."

"Enough." The word seemed to reverberate in the air,

emphasized by Alycia's proper British accent and bitter tone. She glared at me and narrowed her eyes. Ice cold. "How much of the past week do you remember?"

I gave them the CliffsNotes version of the past few days. I conveniently forgot to mention Mort, Dr. Hannigan, and Olivia. Alycia listened carefully and scribbled notes the entire time. I filled them in on how I woke up on the bus, the strange dream of "dying" in the club. The people chasing after me.

"Ah, The Orchid," Pharaoh nodded, showing no change in emotion. "They've been trying to eliminate you ever since you returned."

Even though I already figured my life was in danger, it still sent an icy shiver down my spine. "What, why?"

Alycia looked irritated. "You are guilty of the most extreme case of a time violation we have ever encountered," she spoke fast with venom in her voice. "While The Orchid has immediately deemed you a threat, *Pharaoh* hoped to gain more insight to see just what the hell has happened." Disdain filled her voice, like she disagreed with the decision to keep me alive.

"I don't understand..." I felt like I was going to be sick, a running theme for me lately. "What did I violate? Who the hell are you people?"

Pharaoh leaned forward and set his hands on the table. "Collectively, we identify as *Tempus*. A group of individuals who, for more or less, have gifts outsiders could not understand. We represent The Lotus. The Orchid is another thread of Tempus, one I have had a troubled relationship with. As of a few days ago, you have made yourself known as one of us. And caused a splash in our...ecosystem, for lack of a better word."

"We are divided into several sects, or threads, as Pharaoh mentioned," Quinton added. "They are partly for identification and the names hold little significance now. Knights of this, Order of that, they have changed throughout the centuries. We are all tasked with distinct elements of maintaining the stability of time. And generally speaking, we have coexisted undisturbed. Until you came."

Wow. This was getting confusing. Their words echoed in my head as I tried to piece everything together. So these groups were fighting over me. I was going to get my answers, but by the sounds of it, I started doubting that I'd live long enough to make sense of them.

"This is so—how big is this? Why haven't I heard of this before?" I pondered out loud.

"We have our hands in everything," Quinton said with a knowing smile.

"Yes, *Quinton*," Alycia snapped. "But we do not interfere unless absolutely necessary. We follow our set protocols and vote on any action taken. Now that most civilized society has adopted our models, we just watch, for the most part."

Pharaoh's expression contorted with worry and fear. "But as of late, the protocols have been ignored or outright broken."

"Since I came back?" I attempted to add to the conversation. I still had so many questions, but at least I knew who was chasing me.

"The Orchid has been bending the laws to their liking

before you came." Pharaoh leaned back in his chair. "But yes, since you've returned, they've now completely disregarded them. They've classified you as our prime threat without a formal trial."

"It's hard not to blame them. You wiped out seven years of our lives." Alycia's anger was palpable in the air as she spoke. "Arrogant asshole," she snarled under her breath.

Great, blame the new guy.

"Alycia, please!" Pharaoh's words cut through the air before he turned back to me. "She is unfortunately correct, though. You have set us all back considerable time. After that event you took part in, we have found ourselves in quite the predicament."

So I wasn't alone in this whole time thing. That didn't make me feel much better. "Uh, sorry? I'm not really even sure what I did."

Pharaoh looked deep in thought as he chose his words. "The general population remembers nothing. Mostly. Your case is," he stopped and tapped his fingers together in a rhythmic pattern. "Sensitive."

"And the more intimate your relationship with someone, the more likely they'll have some idea of you. Deep, repressed. They usually come out in dreams or get written off as strange feelings. That's what "déjà vu" is," Quinton said.

"We refer to that as time residue." Pharaoh clasped his hands together and searched for his next words. "Imagine a brain is like a computer's hard drive. Experiences and feelings, data—is constantly being written to it sequentially. Now imagine someone travels back one day in time. The entire world goes back one day with them. Typically, this is of little consequence, as most people relive the same events. Some may experience being *off* temporarily as the brain writes the same data over itself, like Quinton said." I nodded, relieved to find sense in the chaos.

"However, when someone's experiences differ," Pharaoh continued, "Tempus steps in to correct or maintain order, as the data being written is now incongruent. This can cause dangerous alterations to the future, as well as an individual's psyche. Again, this typically results in minor adjustments to the timeline." I saw where this was going.

"Now imagine the world set back seven years by someone in a global spotlight. Your music, movies—everything left a mark on the world causing massive incongruences depending on how deep of an impact you had on the individual. Sadly, it's not unheard of for a select few to remember everything and lose touch with reality. Luckily, we haven't detected significant changes yet, but we are researching how to mitigate the effects as time progresses."

I cringed, then looked down at my lap, wringing my hands a bit too rough while I fought visions of the lives I may had changed.

Pharaoh broke the silence lingering in the room. "In your professional life, you certainly touched a lot of lives. But the deep, emotional connections you made personally will have the greatest effect." He stopped and massaged his temples as if he was afraid to continue. "Did you have any deep relationships—did you *love*?"

My eyes shifted up from my lap. I could feel the heat of Alycia's gaze as she glared at me. "I can't imagine what the hell were you thinking traveling back in your position? And so far?" The anger poured through her words until Pharaoh put his hand on her shoulder. She closed her eyes and appeared to calm down. "You're lucky we didn't join Orchid and end you."

"Alycia, please!" Pharaoh's voice echoed through the room. "Mr. Hagaki, while she doesn't speak for all of us, I will be honest with you. Many are unhappy with your actions. My curiosity and the unknown ramifications of outright killing you have saved your life."

I could only shake my head in disbelief. "I don't *know* what happened. I'm sorry but this is all news to me," I said.

"Likely. It may come back in time, or perhaps you are something of an anomaly," said Pharaoh.

Alycia's words were cold and precise as she spat, "He most definitely *is* an anomaly."

I wanted to ask so many more questions, but my mind was back in overdrive. Some of what they told me made sense now, as my mind was beginning to connect the dots.

"I suppose we should get this over with," Pharaoh said with a business-like tone. He motioned to a cabinet behind him. "It is time to join us. Quinton, scan him in please."

"Sir?" Quinton had a look of concern painted on his face.

"We need to scan him in, of course," Pharaoh said in a harsher tone.

"Sir, with all due respect, we must follow protocol and —" Quinton managed before being cut off.

"The Orchid have been breaking protocol for years. We need him now," Pharaoh demanded.

Quinton slowly stood from the chair and stomped over to the cabinet. He retrieved a small silver device and walked back, pausing in front of me.

"A few decades ago," Pharaoh continued, "we adopted an identification system initially for security and tracking. You've probably seen the most mainstream uses of it now everywhere, from hospitals to your mom and pop grocery stores."

Instinctively, my hand shot to my shoulder. After realizing what I had done, I set my hand down, but it had not gone unnoticed.

"Ah, I see you've found yours," Pharaoh smirked.

Quinton grabbed my hand and pulled my arm forward. He pushed it flush against the table and began rolling up my sleeve. This didn't make sense. Just minutes ago, he had warned me against what he was now about to do. Even if he was following the Pharaoh's orders against his will, I was out of options. Fear set in as I tried to pull my arm free, but he was too strong.

"Hold still please, this will only take a minute!" Quinton struggled to say while holding my arm down.

He continued rolling my sleeve until part of the code showed, now faintly visible. I felt a light pinch on my arm and suddenly his grip loosened. His eyes grew wide as he gave a subtle nod of his head. I jerked my arm up with all my strength, causing him to lose his balance and stumble backward. I shot out of my chair and tore open the conference room doors.

I slammed the door behind me and channeled my energy into sprinting forward. A loud thud boomed from the room behind, as if someone had leapt over the table. With a quick glance back, I saw Alycia chasing behind with Quinton close behind her. Only a few seconds separated us. I rushed fast toward the elevator door, praying it was open.

"You're making a mistake!" Alycia's voice wavered from behind as she tried to keep up. "Stop at once!"

I had no intention of joining some organization right now, even if they were offering me temporary sanctuary. Especially without knowing their true intentions or what they really wanted from me. Part of me felt foolish, but Quinton gave me enough doubt to justify running.

I pushed my legs harder and harder, pounding against the musty old carpet. My lungs and throat were on fire from pushing out so much air. Burning sensations shot through my body, only making me faster. I looked in the distance to see the elevator door was open and waiting for me.

I jumped into the car and in one fluid motion, turned to smash the only button. After tapping the button several times, I stepped back and looked up to see Alycia drawing closer. As the doors inched closer to closing, the sound of metal grating against metal filled the air. Amidst the chaos, I realized I had swiped the silver scanning device. Finding a better use for it, I threw it, aiming for her legs. Direct hit. A leg gave out and she tripped over the little device, crashing forward on her face as tiny silver pieces scattered on the carpet. Quinton jumped over her but miscalculated his landing. He fell awkwardly on her arm causing her to scream in pain.

As the doors closed, I pressed my hand against the console and leaned forward trying to fight the nausea.

22

I fought through the dizziness and took a few deep breaths. Hopefully, this was the only way out. I'd take any advantage I could get. My heart raced as I imagined Alycia powering down a stairwell two steps at a time, already getting into position to greet me.

Now with a moment to myself, I reflected on the conversation. While I felt a strange trust with Quinton, I felt nothing when I met with Pharaoh or Alycia. Why had Quinton aligned with them? He was clearly taking orders, but he seemed strong enough to take care of himself.

The only likely explanation was he had joined the lesser of two evils, if Pharaoh was even evil to begin with. If only they had allowed me some time to think things over before scanning me in. The way they talked about it sounded like a cult. And the idea of doing it against my will was only one of many red flags about the whole situation.

I ran through my mental to-do list, seeing Terrance's

face looming, haunting me from an alternate time. I still wanted to find a way to stop him and save AJ while trying to avoid my new enemies. And then there was Olivia. Time residue or not, they could call it whatever they wanted. I needed to see her again. If I could make it out of this building first.

The door opened bringing me face to face with Quinton. He shook his head at me with a sly smile. "Okay, you have about," he looked down at his watch, "four minutes before Alycia gets down to the ground level."

"Here." He extended his hand, revealing an old flip phone and a set of keys. I grabbed the keys and shoved the phone in my pocket.

"Take my backup. E3 gate forty. Go!" he commanded in a hushed tone.

I dropped the deer in headlights expression and hopped out of the elevator. As I made my way for the exit, he yelled behind me, "She's not a tracker. You should be able to lose her fast."

I bolted out of the room and headed to the first elevator at the end of the hall. I was really getting sick of elevators. It descended much quicker this time, letting me back out into the rainforest that doubled as a lobby. Monica screamed something at me as I ran by and continued down the stairwell to the parking garage.

My lungs still burning from exertion, I took a deep breath and clicked open the garage. Inside sat Quinton's spare. A champagne colored Ferrari with chrome plated wheels. His spare, alright. Luckily I felt quite familiar with it, suddenly remembering I had owned one when I went through my car phase. Would I ever get used to memories of the future?

I turned the ignition and the engine purred to life. The gentle softness disguised the true power under the hood. Backing out in one swift motion, I tore out of the small garage and sped up the levels until I found myself back on the street. I didn't check my rear view, but I imagined I would have seen Alycia in my dust.

I decided I would drive around for a while and think things over before I made any more rash decisions. Why had Quinton led me into the lion's den only to help me escape? If any of the Tempus story was true, there was an underground war going on and I helped stir the pot. Now I only had Quinton as my ally and both sides after me. Instead of falling into another panic, I drove the city streets with the windows down. The warm air streamed through my hair, sending it in every direction.

It was easy for my mind to drift away on the midnight road. I had been in difficult situations before, and from my experience, they didn't end well. Thinking back to my past in China, I searched my memory for anything to help me.

23

———

The trek had taken us days west into the heart of China. While we had prepared for a week's journey, a spat with barbarians set us back an extra day. However, with Yun as my guide, we made up the lost time with a shorter route. The Governor had sent Yun and myself to gather information on the Emperor's plans for our province. For several weeks, rumors made their way to the village from the surrounding areas. The most common being the Emperor had been using any means necessary to overthrow the local leadership in favor of his handpicked men. The locals grew restless.

We were successful in repelling three attacks from the invaders. But each battle came with a cost—lives and morale. And with each attack, the battalion was larger, better equipped, and better trained. It made little sense. Attacks from barbarians were nothing new, but their method hadn't changed for centuries. We were facing a threat unknown to us and we needed answers.

For months the local leadership was promised better

protection, but nothing had been done. Instead, the attacks amplified, leading us to wonder if the Emperor had a hand in this. From everything happening recently, it appeared the rumors were turning out to be true. Our only plan upon reaching the Imperial City was meeting with the Emperor himself.

Tired and worn from traveling, we finally closed on our destination. From our vantage point on the steep hill, we could see the immense city. It spanned for miles with its open fields and beautiful architecture. To guard the citizens from attack, a tall stone barrier protected the entire perimeter. As we drew closer and closer, I realized just how large and detailed the buildings were. I was shocked to learn that people actually lived in the giant works of art.

We walked up to the gate to be greeted by three armored guardsmen, weapons drawn. Two flanked our sides, lances pointed a mere foot from us. The other approached showing no signs of fear. His armor had an extra insignia on it, signifying he had a higher rank than the other two.

"Halt!" He spoke with confidence, holding his palm towards us to stop. "I do not believe you have been authorized for entry."

Yun walked a few steps forward to meet him while I held my ground. He calmly pulled out a scroll and handed it to the senior guard.

"We come with word from Governor Guo, requesting council with the Emperor," said Yun.

The guard unrolled the scroll and read it, taking his time. He raised his eyebrows while reading it, then nodded to the other men. They dropped their weapons and went back to their positions by the gate.

"You are free to enter as guests. By entering the Imperial City you are bound by our law and are expected to follow all policies or face just consequence." He motioned for us to continue in. "When the Emperor is ready, we will find you. However, due to his schedule, you may have to meet with a representative of the senior high council instead."

Yun and I passed each other a knowing nod as we advanced. Our instruction was to meet only with the Emperor. We would not be leaving until he heard from us directly. We already discussed that we had not traveled four days' time to waste it on a council member with his own agenda. With the rumors making their rounds, it was hard to trust anyone's word, council or not.

The sun fell as we ventured further into the city. Beginning to tire, we found a tavern offering reasonable rates. The Governor made sure we had plenty of coin for our journey, but we thought it best not to advertise that fact. I found the room pleasant even though I slept on the floor. Despite his protests, I made Yun take the elegant cloth bed. I looked out the small window to see we were near the Emperor's Palace. I hoped we could meet with him soon and get back on our way home.

Two days passed before we received a knock on our door. A short, balding man stood at the door.

He spoke in a low voice, causing me to lean in to listen. "You are very lucky. The Emperor has agreed to meet with you."

I was elated after two days of waiting. "Thank you. When is our meeting?"

"He is awaiting your company now."

I woke Yun and we both were ready within minutes. We followed the short man towards the Palace. He took a sudden, sharp turn leading in the opposite direction.

I could sense Yun's suspicions raised as well.

"Almost there," his voice wavered as we hurried behind him. His head swiveled as if he was lost or looking for something.

I slowed my pace and whispered to Yun. "Something's not right here."

He looked around the dark alley we had found ourselves in and nodded that he agreed. I felt uneasy knowing I had left my weapons in the room, but bringing them would be an impolite gesture to the Emperor. I now wished I had at least taken a dagger as the man led us further away from the Palace.

The short man came to a complete stop and turned around. He spoke loudly even though we were a mere feet away. "I'm sorry, I guess I must be *a bit lost*, heh heh." The cackling laughter revealed his yellow, decaying teeth.

As soon as he finished talking, a man dressed in black robes emerged from the shadows. "I think you've gone far enough," the mysterious man said.

Two large guards appeared behind him, dressed in the same dark armor as the invaders we had encountered in the past weeks.

"A season of change is upon us," the robed figure said. "Do not deny it grows closer." The voice had a charismatic quality that drew me in with each word. "The Emperor is weak, ignorance clouding his vision."

The figure reached into a deep pocket within the robe and revealed a tattered scroll. "We grow stronger each day." With the scroll unraveled, the figure stepped closer, still shadowed in darkness. A pale shriveled hand presented the parchment. "Join us. Join the birth of a new dynasty."

So not only were the rumors true, but we now had a chance to join the enemy haunting the village. The evil emanating from the figure overpowered logic, causing me to battle the urge to grab the scroll.

Yun must have noticed my internal struggle and spoke in a commanding tone, directed both at me and the figure. "We will never join you. We swear our allegiance to our Emperor!"

"Very well. Your pathetic village is already ours. Crushed, just as all who stand in the way of my holy rule. The Empire will be mine," the robed figure said as he motioned his bodyguards to move forward. He turned and began to walk away. "If you'll excuse me, I have more pressing matters to attend to."

The short man ran after him, leaving us with the guards. Force of habit caused me to grab at where my sword typically hung, only to come back empty-handed. The burly men drew their weapons in unison. One equipped with a sword, the other a flail. In my peripheral vision, I saw Yun search himself as well. I returned my focus to the flail welder, who began swinging wildly with a look of pleasure on his face.

The attacker launched the spiked ball at my torso,

grazing my abdomen as I leapt backward. He swung again, using the momentum to repeat the same offense. I fell to the ground, dodging the attack, and rolled over out of range.

Yun had found a dagger and was dodging attacks from the other guard, his weapon clearly no match. I sprang to my feet and regained my balance. My attacker swung several more times, each slightly closer until I was backed against the side of a building. He laughed, realizing I was cornered, then launched the spike towards me with all his might. At just the right moment, I dropped to the side and out of its way. It struck the wall with a deafening thud, scattering broken stone across the ground.

The impact's vibration caused him to drop the weapon and reactively tend to his hand. I picked up the flail and without hesitation, swung at his head. The heavy spiked ball connected with his helmet and knocked him into the dirt. I pulled hard at the flail to retrieve the metal ball, but it was embedded deep in the fallen guard's helmet. I propped my foot on his chest as leverage to muscle it out.

I readied to strike again when I noticed the guard's mangled helmet and bloodied face. Several of the spikes had gone through his armor making my single swing a fatal blow. I looked over to see Yun still fending off the sword attacks—making little progress to slow his attacker.

I ran behind the other guard and launched the flail one more time, hitting his neck hard. He screamed in pain and fell to his knees. Yun launched at the guard's exposed neck with his dagger and the screaming stopped within seconds.

After recuperating from the battle, it had become obvious that someone within the Emperor's council, if not the Emperor himself, had been behind the attacks on the village.

Out of breath and bleeding from my gut, I stood to face Yun. "What now?"

"We must get to the Emperor." Yun bent down and grabbed a bloody helmet off the ground and walked away with a slight limp.

"And what if he's the one behind all this?" I lashed back.

He stopped, looking back at me before continuing. "Then we fight until we die," Yun said, with a stoic expression.

I nodded. There was no way to win against the power of the Emperor's army. It was a lost cause, but I would still fight until the end. As we backtracked towards the Palace, I hoped that wasn't the case.

24

———————

We walked up the Palace stairs until two of the Emperor's Guard stopped us. Like the others we had seen before in the city, they were wearing the standard issue steel armor. Unlike the guards we had encountered earlier. They looked down to see Yun holding a bloodied helmet and readied their weapons.

"Come no further!" The guard's voice was gruff and authoritative.

Yun defied the order and walked closer to the doors. "We are here for council with the Emperor."

The guard readied to strike. "Set your weapons down at once!" Fire burned in his eyes.

Yun and I exchanged a knowing look and complied. We laid our weapons on the stone ground and backed away.

The other guard stepped forward and joined the conversation. "Murder of Shing Han's personal guard is an attack on the advisor himself!"

"These men attacked us. They wish to stop our meeting with the Emperor. We have been summoned." Yun said with desperation, now showing signs of the battle.

Yun pulled the Governor's letter from his pocket. He took small steps as he approached the guard and surrendered it with a trembling hand. The guard looked it over and, much to our amazement, the giant doors soon opened. He led us through the entire Palace until we reached the Emperor's chambers.

He stopped, his hand on the handle. "All is not well here." An eerie stillness hung in the air. "There have been rumblings that Shing Han wishes to overthrow the Emperor's rule."

I could sense Yun felt the same relief I did after hearing that. If this was true, I hoped this meant the Emperor was not behind the recent attacks at the village. I feared we might have run out of time to do something about Shing Han, or whoever it was, as they had already extended their reign far into our land.

The guard cautiously opened the door to the Emperor's Chambers. Candles flickered in the immense room filled with gold and silk. In the distance sat the Emperor, accompanied by the dark robed figure at his side. Several others were also in the room, working on various projects.

"Emperor!" the guard said as he bowed. We followed his lead.

"Rise," the Emperor commanded, his voice booming through the room.

The robed man stood to his feet. "What is the meaning of this intrusion?"

As we walked closer, Yun threw the bloody helmet, which landed in a loud clash in front of the Emperor. "You sent your men to kill us, Shing Han! To stop us from telling the Emperor of the blood bath you've caused in our—"

His sentence was abruptly cut off by Shing's rage-filled shout. "That is absurd!"

Yun appeared unfazed by Shing and continued. "Your highness, that man that stands next to you is a traitor to the—"

Shing's voice cut through again. "Guards, take these liars away at once!"

"No." The Emperor spoke with confidence. "Let him finish, Shing."

I caught the smallest exhale of relief from Yun before he spoke. "I come from the Province of Jiangsu, village of Huaxi. For months, we have fought invaders dressed in that very armor before your feet."

"Lies!" Shing clasped his hands and twirled his thumbs. "You cannot trust these men! More of the twisted tongue, your highness."

"Let him speak, Shing. Do not interrupt him again."

We walked closer to them, now just a short distance away.

"Shing's men just attacked us outside the Palace. He plans to overthrow the Empire, your highness!" I admired Yun's courage in moments like these. He had been a great teacher over the years.

The Emperor grew quiet, his gaze lingering on Shing.

"This is not the first time I have heard this accusation, Shing Han." The Emperor's voice trembled with rage for the first time.

With my nerves beginning to calm, I chimed in, "We speak the truth, your highness."

The Emperor spoke, now louder in his command. "Shing Han, as of now I—"

Before he could finish, Shing launched at the Emperor and plunged a dagger into him. He missed the intended mark and hit the Emperor's right shoulder. Blood pooled at the wound as Shing pulled out the blade and thrust into him again. The Emperor screamed and tried to push him off as Shing readied for a third stab.

Yun caught Shing's arm, causing them both to tumble to the marble floor. I ran to the Emperor to tend to his wounds while Yun freed the weapon from Shing's grasp.

Several guards ran into the room after I yelled for help. The guards pulled Shing from the floor and dragged him away, hopefully to a dungeon below. Yun remained unshaken, even after catching the blade during the struggle. The Emperor winced in pain as the warm, sticky blood oozed down his body. He breathed a soft "Thank you" before the guards carried him away.

WE SPENT the next days exploring the city and making connections with local traders and laborers. Rebuilding the village would come at a cost and thankfully the Emperor provided us each with coin for our service. As time passed, I hoped Yun had forgotten my lapse in judgement—the pull towards Shing's words. Our last night in the city, I broke through my embarrassment as we prepared to leave.

"His words...I felt a hold on me like I have never known."

Yun continued gathering our supplies, readying to leave. "With age comes experience. I've taught you to build your body—but you must now fortify your mind."

I nodded. His words made sense, but I had no idea what that sort of training would entail.

"While Shing's proposition was enticing, remember everyone has their own agenda. Even the Emperor. What I said back there about allegiance—we must do what's best for ourselves, above all. Sometimes the best option is you."

I bit my lip, puzzled at the new lesson.

Yun smiled, the look he often had after teaching me a new technique. "Don't forget your coin, it's time to leave."

I grabbed the small coin pouch, tracing the white blossom etched in the fabric before stowing it away in my satchel.

25

A soft tone dinged and the low fuel light appeared on the dash. I realized I had been driving around for over an hour and a half and Quinton hadn't called yet. And I was running out of ideas on where to go. Without even thinking, my daydreaming car ride had taken me only a few miles away from the motel.

I needed to know if Olivia was okay, but the motel was probably the first place Alycia or the suits would look. The urge to be with her again overruled logic. I convinced myself it wouldn't hurt to check the area to make sure everything looked okay.

I crept past the motel parking lot and looked for anything suspicious. No silver BMW, but the area looked busier than I had remembered. The manager's office was closed off by yellow police caution tape, most likely because of a certain anonymous tip. Serves the pig right.

As I was about to leave, I noticed a phone company van parked by the stairwell to the second floor. Normally this wouldn't make me think twice. But it was after midnight and the strange situation around the mysterious phone upgrade had me questioning. I was already on edge from the past day's events, even more so after learning of a shadowy organization hot on my trails. My paranoia mixed with the yearning to see her. I justified taking a risk to find out if she was in danger.

Walking right in wasn't the smartest idea. I needed to find another way to get to her. Remembering I had Quinton's cell phone, I started dialing the number I saw earlier on my room's phone but changed the last two digits to her room number. To my surprise, it worked and the line started ringing.

It rang three times until Olivia answered with hesitation in her voice. "H-Hello?"

"Hi Olivia, I'm sorry if I woke you. It's Hagaki, from earlier tonight."

I heard rustling around until she answered a few seconds later. "I'm so glad you called." She sounded concerned.

"Is everything okay?"

"Yeah, I'm fine. But a few minutes after you left the bar, a couple of guys came in and started looking everyone up and down. They didn't say anything, just left after a few minutes. It was really creepy and reminded me of something out of a sci-fi movie."

I thought of the suits from the museum. Possibly from the Orchid group, I had learned.

"Oh wow, that's bizarre."

"They were after you, weren't they? That man who took you..." Her voice trembled.

"He's an old friend," I lied.

"He was in my dream too, Hagaki. He came to take you away from them, didn't he?"

"It's a long story. I'm sorry..." I trailed off, hoping to avoid answering.

"Why, what happened?"

"I didn't want to get you mixed up in this. I think they're watching you," I paused, half-regretting I had stopped to see her. "I'm so sorry."

The phone was silent long enough to make me uncomfortable until she answered. I knew she hadn't hung up because I heard her breathing lightly.

"I need to get you out of there, Olivia."

After another long pause, she finally answered. Much more calmly than I expected. "I'm ready."

"Can you run?" I asked.

"If my life depends on it," she said with a sarcastic edge.

"Good. They're in the parking lot now. A van, I think. Take the stairwell that wraps around the building and goes away from the road. I'm parked at the gas station two blocks over. Black car, tinted windows."

"See ya soon."

I finished filling the tank and paid with a few bills from the heavy money clip I found in the car's center console. I pocketed the rest, Quinton would have to take an IOU. The nervous feeling in my stomach grew with every minute that my rear view mirror was empty. Trying to fight jumping to the worst conclusion, I started second guessing the entire plan. Maybe I could have just driven right up to her room and sped away. I could have outrun that van. Or maybe I should have tried to slash its tires first. Or not even tell her. She wasn't a threat to them.

The thoughts faded as I saw her approaching. She pulled the passenger door open and slammed it hard after sinking into the seat. I pressed on the gas a little too hard and the car jerked forward. After a few seconds, I got a handle on the speed and we were zooming off towards the freeway.

Olivia panted hard to catch her breath. She looked like she was going to vomit until she reached into her purse and pulled out an inhaler. She took two puffs and soon her breathing slowed. I divided my attention between her, the road, and my mirrors. No signs of the van or anyone following us, but they weren't easy to lose.

Once on the freeway, I floored the gas causing the engine to roar loudly. I realized just how fast the car was after seeing my speedometer top 100 in a matter of seconds. Easing off the pedal, I balanced the speed to match the limit.

She settled into her seat after catching her breath and looked over at me with a crooked smile. "Nice car."

Her response took me by surprise. "Thanks, but it's not mine. Too flashy." I beamed a smile, glad she made it safely before reality sank in. "I'm really sorry Olivia. I can't say it enough."

"I have to ask. Those dreams I told you about..." she said with confidence I hadn't seen in her.

"Yeah?"

"They aren't just dreams, are they? They feel like memories, but we're older in them."

I sat in silence as we sped down the freeway. I didn't

know how much I should tell her or if I should say anything at all. But I owed it to her. To let her know why she was even with me right now.

"I—" I took a deep breath, "I have these memories, they're my past but not the me you see. I've always had them. But now, I'm seeing things from the future. Everything is different."

In my peripheral vision, she turned to me, hanging on my words.

"Yeah? Like what?" she asked.

I made my best attempt to explain the dream I had. A reality that started when I arrived in California, but led me down such a different path. How she was in the dream, too. That everything synced up with what she told me until it ended with the gunshot in the club. That I remembered darkness until I woke up back on the bus with her next to me. I left out my meeting with Quinton, deciding I would gauge her reaction so far.

"So you're telling me these dreams, these visions..." She waited for me to fill in the blank.

"They're..." I whispered, pausing.

"They're real?"

I caught a glimpse of the confusion on her face. We let the silence take over again. I remembered Quinton looking at my bar code when he found me at the bar. He could tell if I was being tracked by the color of it. I looked to find it had no color and was barely visible. I hoped that meant that I was no longer being tracked and took the next exit off the freeway.

"We should find somewhere to sleep for the night. Make some sense of this?"

She nodded without saying a word. She had time to think about her dreams, but the idea of them being a reality was just sinking in. I figured it would be best to let her think things over first instead of adding to her confusion.

Off the freeway, I found a row of expensive looking hotels. I picked the largest one and made sure to back into my parking spot to avoid someone scanning the license plate. While the car was expensive and uncommon, it fit in with all the rare and foreign models in the lot.

Olivia followed me into the hotel, still silent. The lobby was empty, thanks to being well into the night. We had the entire elegant lobby to ourselves. A large chandelier hung from the ceiling next to several tall pillars of marble. The floor looked to be made of marble with gold trim that sparkled with each step we took. She had a faint smile on her face as we walked up to the receptionist at the front desk.

"Hello there, Sir, Madame," she said, her voice monotone.

"Hello. My wife and I are looking for a room tonight. We had planned to stay with a relative, but unfortunately plans fell through."

The receptionist looked us over with what looked like disgust and started typing at her machine.

"We are all out of rooms. I'm sorry sir," she said, still staring at the screen.

I pulled out my car keys and set them on the counter, letting the Ferrari logo crash hard on the marble. She saw the keys and looked away from the monitor.

"Are you sure they are all taken? Any room will do." I smiled and peered into her eyes, connecting in an intense but comforting way.

Her face flashed with embarrassment and her mood lightened. "Oh, I'm sorry." She pretended to type away again. "We have one room available. It's a suite on the eighteenth floor. Seven hundred per night, sir."

"Perfect!" I pulled out nine hundred-dollar bills and placed seven of them in front of her. "You know, our luck has been terrible today. They lost our luggage with all our clothes and identification. I hope this can cover any deposit?" I slid two hundred-dollar bills towards her.

She caught on to my bribe. I knew a place like this wouldn't let just anyone waltz right in. It's best to cut them off before they even have a chance to ask.

"Of course, sir," she said, sliding the bills off the counter and down to her pocket.

She grabbed our key from below the counter. I thanked her and Olivia followed me to the elevator. As soon as the elevator doors closed, Quinton's phone rang.

RE: OLIVIA

My life had changed in just a matter of days. I watched the doors close at a snail's pace, staring forward, unable to break my gaze. The strange jingle broke me out of the trance.

"Quinton?" he answered with desperation in his voice.

I heard some chatter from the earpiece, too distorted to make anything out.

His face relaxed a bit. "Yeah. I'm okay. I think I lost them. I'm at—" Cut off by more muffled speech.

"Understood, so...Hello? Hello?" He took the phone away from his ear and checked the display.

"Damn," he said to himself. "No reception in this metal box."

"Who was that?" I asked, even though I already knew it was the man from earlier tonight.

"My friend. Well, I'm pretty sure he's a friend. He's been helping me."

The elevator stopped and opened to our floor. We continued walking towards our hotel room. He went first, with extreme caution and a very slow pace.

"The man from the bar?" I asked.

"Yeah." We stopped in front of our door and he slid the key card through the reader. As he opened the door, I put my hand on his shoulder, stopping him from going in.

"Who is he?"

He turned to face me with a somber look on his face. "He's part of some agency, I think. I'm still figuring out the details, but I don't know if I can trust him. I feel like I know him, but we haven't met before today." He looked around the hallway and motioned for me to follow.

I shut the door behind me and leaned my back against it. Even though it was his fault for getting me involved, this felt like it was meant to happen. And I wanted to be by his side. It was a hell of a lot more interesting than what I had going on before.

"Why are those men chasing you? What happened at that party?" I asked, with my back still against the door.

In my dreams, the party ended with an ambulance arriving and paramedics saving him from the gunshot. His version didn't line up. Was he talking about time travel? Somehow we had the same story until that gunshot, but I had a feeling we both might be right. And in my last dream, things repeated. I remember feeling like I had a second chance at...something.

"You'd think I'm even crazier if I told you," he whispered.

I walked towards him and looked deep into his blue eyes. Electricity ran through my body like the first time I saw him in that store. I fought the urge to kiss him and took a step back. He looked away for a moment after realizing how close we were. Was he nervous?

I waited until he looked back and our eyes met. "Please."

"That man... After we left, he took me to meet someone. They said I changed the course of time. After I was shot, like in your dream—they said I set things back seven years. I don't get it. It's all so unbelievable. I feel like I'm still dreaming."

I sat on the bed and wondered how this could have happened. Maybe I was losing it. Do people realize when they are hallucinating? I came to Cali to get away from the stress of everyday life. My therapist thought this vacation would be a good idea. So many thoughts filled my head. I wanted to pull my hair out. So much for a vacation. He must have noticed the look on my face.

"Hey, don't worry. He's going to call me back soon," he said, looking over at me with calm from the other side of the room. "We're gonna figure this out, okay?"

I nodded, wiping the single tear from my eye and laid down on the bed. He disappeared into the bathroom and I heard him start the water. I must have dozed off for a few minutes because I woke to the shower door closing. The bathroom door opened, releasing steam into the air as he walked out in only a towel around his waist.

He was lean and pretty muscular, which took me by

surprise. His baggy clothes hid it well. I sat upright to see him walk towards the mirror.

"Bathroom's all steamy, sorry," he said while trimming his beard. His wet hair looked much darker and longer. I stood up and looked over his shoulder, fixated on the mirror. Near his shoulder blade I saw a three inch scar. Exactly where he was shot in my dreams. In just a single moment, my fears of going crazy, my doubts that I was hallucinating—they all vanished. The connection with him was real.

I sauntered up behind him. He glanced up at the mirror, meeting his eyes with mine.

"If those dreams I'm having are real..." I processed out aloud, searching for the words somewhere on his body.

He turned around to face me and put down his scissors.

"Then it means everything that happened between us..." I paused again. My fingers ran down his cheek with the softest touch. I continued until I reached the scar on his shoulder. "Was real."

He looked down at the scar and put his hand over it. I saw his vulnerability looking up at me. My brain tingled, deep into my mind. We stood there, lost in each other's eyes, sharing the same revelation.

He exhaled and pulled me in tight. His lips tasted so familiar against mine. I put my hands around his back and kissed him harder. His hands grabbed my hips and pulled me against him. He knew his way around my body like I knew his. He pulled back for just a moment and smiled back at me.

Leaning in closer, he whispered into my ear. "I don't think you were dreaming."

So cheesy. I love cheesy.

26

A horrible rumble came from the nightstand. I jolted out of bed, grabbing the phone and flipping it open against my ear. I would have to get used to flip phones again.

"H-Hello?"

I rubbed my fingers over my eyes to clear the sleep. The green glow from the nightstand said it was 3 in the morning. Olivia was sound asleep on the other side of the bed with only a sheer silk blanket covering her body. She looked so peaceful. Looking at her put a huge smile on my face. Everything I had felt about her was right.

"Hagaki? Hello?" Quinton's frantic tone tore me from the daydream. Or maybe I was falling back asleep on my feet.

"I'm here."

"I was following their communications. The trackers got wind of you, but you lost them. No easy feat but I'm sure my car helped with that," he laughed.

"It didn't hurt. What do I do now?"

"I'd rather not tell you this over the phone, but we have little time. They tasked me with watching you and bringing you in when the time was right, but I never thought they would try to initiate you. I couldn't let you get scanned back there because then you'd link with Lotus. Orchid has been watching their every move. If you were to be scanned under Pharaoh, Orchid would revolt. Orchid revolts, our entire system fails. Our instability causes society's instability."

"Who thought I'd be so important? Wouldn't I have protection from them after being scanned?"

"Normally yes. When a traveler gets scanned, they receive a certain amount of immunity. But they have to go in front of the Tempus council before it's made official."

"I don't understand."

"The normal process involves a traveler such as yourself going in front of our governing body. Then you choose your alignment officially. And in theory, all is well and done. Tempus is steeped in rigid tradition. That is partly why we've been unknown for centuries."

"Then why is Orchid trying to kill me?"

"Orchid is overstepping their boundaries. You are an anomaly. Typically travelers shift a day or week at most, and then we find them. We've never seen someone travel back as far as you. Nobody knows your limits. And your celebrity status has affected thousands, maybe millions. Orchid is threatened. If they kill you, they will be breaking our code, but it will eventually blow over since they plan to write it off as for the greater good. If Pharaoh scans you in, Orchid will fight back. Both sects have enough power to crash the stock markets, crumble economies, start world wars."

"Then what do I do? Why can't they leave me alone?"

"The Lotus sees you as restoring the balance. They will stop at nothing to ally you with them, officially or not. There is a third option, however."

"I'm listening."

Olivia rolled over and saw me standing by the door on the phone. "Hagaki? Where are you?"

I cupped my hand over the phone, "Right here, Liv. I think it's good news." Liv. It came out naturally, but still sounded foreign.

"Who is that?" Quinton raised his voice.

"The girl from the bar, she knew about me, about what happened before I came back!" I heard Olivia perk up and sit up against the bed's headboard.

"You've put her in danger as well, but if she has information, it may help us understand more. We need to keep her safe until you meet at the quarterly."

"How am I supposed to meet with them if everyone wants a piece of me? What is this third option?"

"If you meet directly with the Tempus council, you can choose neutrality. It is quite rare, but in this case, it is our only choice."

Our. Finally something to give me optimism. "I can't just walk right in there, can I?"

"Think of the Council meeting ground as an embassy, sanctuary, holy ground—"

"Okay, Okay. I get it." I looked over to see Olivia alert and listening to the conversation.

"We need to get you there safely. Once you are there, I can take care of the rest."

"And after? Won't they just kill me then?"

"No. We are bound by laws higher than morality and the judgment system you are accustomed to. Right now you're fair game since you're not aligned. Thats why Orchid is so persistent."

"And what if I choose my own way, Quinton?" Anger rose inside me. "What if I choose to run, or to fight, or what if I choose nothing? I don't know how I feel about joining in all of this."

"They will find you wherever you go. They will kill or capture you. I can't force you to do this, but there's more at stake than just you. I'm going to call back in half an hour. I hope you will be ready to leave. You can't run forever. "

The paced breathing helped calm my nerves. I spoke with a child-like whimper, "Quinton?"

"Yes?"

"Why are you doing this?"

"We need to restore order and," he paused for a few beats. "I know I can trust you."

I leaned back against the wall as the phone went silent.

"So he finally called?" Olivia asked, signs of sleepiness in her voice. She stretched her arms out and yawned. I couldn't help but smile.

"Yeah. We're going to fix this. All of this. He's calling back soon. We need to get ready."

27

I threw on my clothes and sat back on the bed. Where could I begin processing what Quinton told me? My mood changed from hopeful to despair. Olivia finished dressing and sat next to me. It must have been obvious my mood had changed. She placed her hand on my knee and looked at me.

"Hey, talk to me." She kept her gaze, but I continued staring at the floor.

I locked my head in a slouched position. I was really just trying to avoid looking into those eyes. Even if she was somehow involved, I had made her a target. It was too easy to beat myself up over it. Now I had to join some kind of cult not to get killed, and who knows what would happen to her after.

"Hey!" she raised her voice. "Why won't you even look at me? I heard half of the conversation, you know. I'm not stupid. I filled in the blanks."

No, I knew she wasn't stupid at all. I'd bet she played

naïve to get out of awkward situations, though. Or maybe she was the kind of girl that enjoyed creating them, just to see you squirm. But right now, she saw right through me. I could see why I fell for her once already. I pulled my head up to focus on those green eyes.

"My life has been far from normal. I've made peace with that," I said.

Living out my past life in China was something that I used to my advantage and had benefited from. But it took years to adjust to that knowledge in my current life. It wasn't easy. The curiosity had battled inside my mind for so long until it gave up. I could never make much sense of why or how I remembered. But I eventually embraced it instead of letting myself dwell on questions I couldn't answer. I had gotten so far without knowing and as each year passed, I cared less about why. I felt safe in my cocoon of ignorance, protecting me from whatever secrets I may possess in my mind.

Until the dreams rattled the cage, waking up whatever thoughts were sleeping within me. And this time, they came back tenfold. My only glimmer of hope—maybe this Tempus council could answer some of the questions. The ones I had rightfully buried years ago, fearing the answers would change my life even more.

"But this," I looked at her again. "This just makes things more complicated."

She stood up and looked down at me. For the first time, I saw anger on her face.

"Complicated? I've been having dreams about a time traveling stranger that turn out to be memories, I think.

And now he ends up getting me mixed up with people giving him free cars and trying to kill him. That's complicated."

"You don't understand."

"You said we can fix this. That's exactly what we're gonna do!"

I admired her passion. I needed that to boost me back up. Her words were like kindling dropped on the tiny fire burning within me. My mind cleared, making way for more logic. I've had a long, fucked up life, and I mean that in the best way. I guess I needed a reminder to roll with whatever it throws at me.

I stood up at her and smiled, nodding in agreement. "He said I need to get to some kind of embassy where I'll be safe from them. If we can reach it, they won't be able to hurt us anymore."

"Ever?"

"That's what he said." I shrugged. "I know it doesn't make a lot of sense, but the only other options we have are to die fighting or run forever."

"Can you trust him? What if it's a trap?"

"He's already helped me escape a few times today. He had his chance to hurt us earlier if he wanted to."

She turned around and started towards the window. Her hand opened the blinds and she glanced down below.

"You know," she said, her eyes fixed on the ground outside the window, "I tried killing myself before I decided to leave home." She played with the blinds, swaying them back and forth in a rhythm. "I slit my wrist and sat in the bathtub. My sister came to visit a day early from college and found me passed out. If she was only a few minutes—" she stopped and closed her eyes for a moment.

I almost interrupted the silence, but realized she wanted me to listen.

She traced the scar with her fingers. "I didn't really want to die. I just was tired of not living. I wasn't unhappy, I was just bored. They called it a rut, but it lasted four years." She exhaled and shook her head. "What I'm trying to say is, I guess I wanted life to be like a movie. Or at least I wanted more out of life. I dreamed of being zapped out of my dull reality and having a reason to live. A purpose."

I stood silent and motionless, still looking at her back as she resumed playing with the blinds.

"Sorry if this sounds all so sudden, but being with you, seeing all of this, I realize I was already living. I just never took the time to appreciate every day I was alive. I mean, it sounds silly but, fuck. Just getting out of bed in the morning. Not everyone gets to do that." She took a long, heavy drag of air before exhaling with a peaceful smile across her face.

I realized she was the silver lining in this entire situation. No, the golden, the platinum. Hell, she was a diamond. Beat that for cheesy. No matter how bad things got, how close to death I was, she was with me now. I had helped her in some backwards way I never expected, and it put some life back in me.

She sighed and turned her head to face me. I caught

the joy on her face before she turned back to the parking lot.

Her voice trembled as she leaned closer to the window. "Uhhhh...you better look at this...."

28

───────

I ran over to the window and looked down at the parking lot.

"There," Olivia said, pointing at a black SUV creeping in the dim light.

I almost told her she was overreacting until the flashes of light beamed off the other cars as it passed. The lights bounced up and down both sides of the aisle in a systematic pattern.

"Think that's for us?" she whispered, both of us still studying the light show.

"If it is, they wouldn't be stupid enough to give themselves away unless..." I paused to scratch my beard, thinking aloud, "they had a second team on their way up right now."

The jarring vibration of the phone startled me, almost enough for me to lose my train of thought.

I flipped it open to hear a frantic Quinton screaming in my ear. "Hagaki, get out. Get out now. They've got a lock on you."

"Where? I see them in the lot searching the cars."

More rustling in the background. "You're at the Carlyle Towers, shit. I'm listening to their broadcasts. They're both on to you now, coming up fast."

"Both? What now? How am I supposed to get out of here?"

"Well." More chatter interrupted from his radio. "From the sounds of it, in a body bag or with Alycia. Have her capture you. That should give us enough time. At least she'll try to keep you alive, I hope." His engine roared, forcing me to pull the phone from my ear. "I'm almost there, but it'll be too late."

"There has to be another way. When I get out, where do I meet you?"

"You can't fight them Hagaki! Orchid will kill you before you get a chance. And Alycia is authorized to use lethal force if need be."

I walked over to the door and pulled it open. I popped my head out into the hallway and made sure it was clear before motioning for Olivia to follow. She kept close as we jogged down the hallway towards the stairs.

"Just tell me where to meet you!" I said, while scanning the surroundings.

"Hollywood Cemetery. The Pillbrook Mausoleum. Once you're past the cemetery gates, you'll be safe. But we need to get you—" The line went dead.

I slipped the phone in my pocket and opened the stairwell door. Hopefully I didn't miss anything too important from Quinton, but I had more pressing things to focus on now. Inside the stairwell, the loud pounding of footsteps echoed from the floors below. They grew louder as I saw Alycia powering up the stairs two at a time.

I slammed the door shut and ran back to the elevators. Olivia pressed the button to descend on each of the three consoles. Above the car doors, the display showed both the middle and right elevators were ascending fast. The left car was descending, but skipped floor eighteen. Still waiting while both cars raced to our floor, Alycia crashed open the stairwell door and sprinted towards us —the eighteen floors of climbing hadn't phased her one bit.

She was only twenty feet away from us when the first elevator opened. The two suited Orchid men we saw earlier emerged, looking first at us and then at the other end of the corridor to Alycia. Without slowing, she continued running and then leapt into the air. With an amazing show of acrobatics, her leg extended, causing her foot to slam in hard into one of the suited man's ribs.

At the same moment, the other man's fist caught her neck as she fell toward the ground and soon crumpled into a ball. She clutched her neck with both hands, coughing violently and backing away from the man, who turned his attention to us. The other man sat up against the wall, grabbing his side, wincing in pain.

The man pulled out a gun from his suit jacket and fired straight at me. Time melted away in front of my eyes. The bullet cut through the air with a sharp whistling sound, but it felt like an eternity until it came near. I took advantage of the delay and pulled Olivia's wrist hard. We collapsed on the floor as the bullet whizzed over us. The man lowered the gun and approached, stopping near point blank range.

Alycia kicked in his left knee from behind. He moved to correct his balance, only to topple over backwards on to the other man tending his ribs. Alycia then turned her attention to me and started inching closer, only to have her foot grabbed by the man still trying to make his way up from the floor.

As she turned around to face him, I jumped up and pulled Olivia into the elevator. I pushed the lobby button hard and after a few painful seconds, the doors started to close. Before shutting, I caught a glimpse of Alycia fighting the suited man who was clearly losing the battle.

While the elevator slowly lowered towards the lobby, Olivia turned to me with an uneasy look on her face.

"Why were they fighting?"

I took a moment to catch my breath and looked over at her. "One group wants me dead, one wants me captured. I don't want either."

"How are we going to get out? They're watching the car."

I shot a faint smile. "Borrow another one?" Her expression didn't change, unsure if I was serious or not. I wasn't sure myself, but it seemed like the only option now.

As the elevator lowered past the eleventh floor, I prepared myself for whatever temight be behind the doors. Instead, a loud crash erupted from the top of the elevator, shaking it violently. The lights flickered as Olivia was thrown to the ground hard while I slammed into the side of the wall.

The car slowed for a moment and then continued

descending at a normal pace. A few seconds later, it slowed again, this time coming to a complete halt on the third floor. The lights flickered faster, causing me to shield my eyes from the strobe effect.

"Do you—hear something?" Olivia asked as she pulled herself up with the guardrails.

I raised my chin and focused above us. There was a harsh, metallic sound as something strained from above. The lights went out, leaving us in the darkness while the sound got louder. The noise evolved into what sounded like the ceiling being punched.

My heart was pounding as I ran my fingers through my hair, trying to make sense of the unfamiliar sounds.

"She's above us."

29

Without hesitation, I jammed my fingers in between the elevator doors and pulled as hard as I could. The doors barely gave way while my shoulders and triceps began to burn. It wasn't until Olivia pressed the red emergency button that the doors finally moved. Work smart, not hard, I guess. I pushed the doors to the edges until they clicked, locking in place.

The noises from the top of the car only grew louder. I glanced up and saw the small metal grate buckling inward from being hit repeatedly. Through the grate, I caught sight of Alycia's boot pounding it.

I focused my attention back towards getting out. The elevator had stopped somewhere between the third and fourth floors, not aligned with the outer doors. I crouched down and hoped these doors would open just as easy. Blood rushed into my arms while I leaned in, pressing even harder. They squealed open, exposing a hallway like the one we came from. Unfortunately, these doors didn't lock into place.

Alycia was ready to break through at any moment, giving us little time to move. After a second of apprehension, Olivia crawled out between the opening. Not wasting a moment, she reached in and held one of the inner doors back, giving me enough time to snake my body between the opening. I landed softly on the carpet below while the doors closed hard behind me.

As soon as my feet touched the ground, the grate inside the car shattered. With one last burst of energy, I pulled one of the doors open and pushed myself forward to give myself a longer reach.

"Hold it open," I said to Olivia.

I stretched my arm as far as I could and pressed the highest floor button, then managed to hit the stop button so the car would resume its regular functions. I fell backwards and let go of the door, causing me to slam down hard. I looked up at the lights above the door and sighed, relieved the see the elevator was now ascending.

"That probably bought us another minute. Let's go," I said.

We ran towards the stairwell and raced down until we reached the lobby. Now at our destination, more suited men waited near the elevators on the other side of the building. They were expecting us from the elevator, standing with their backs to us. We walked briskly towards the front exit, hoping not to jar their vision in our direction. We stepped outside and looked across the lot, the acrid smell of cigarette smoke drifting from the valet booth where a man stood puffing away.

"Distract the valet. I'm going to get a car."

Olivia nodded and walked towards the attendant. "Sir?" she said in an innocent tone.

He walked away from his booth and started talking to her. I slipped by them and reached into the cupboard inside the booth, my fingers brushing against the cold metal of the keys in the unlocked box. Olivia continued her conversation as I walked away towards the parking lot. I pocketed two of the key rings and started hitting the lock button on each with my thumbs. The first car that chirped was a large SUV. I continued walking until the second car beeped.

I ditched the SUV key and hopped into the flashy sports car. While the SUV could take more damage, right now I needed speed. The engine roared as I turned the key, sounding almost as powerful as Quinton's Ferrari.

I drove back near the entrance to see Olivia walking towards me. She looked behind her and then darted in a full sprint towards the car and jumped in.

"Go!"

She didn't have to tell me twice. I slammed on the gas and peeled out of the parking lot onto the main road. "She just came out of the elevator. Those men are fighting her!"

"Hopefully they'll keep her busy for a while," I said with a smile.

I sped down the dark road, having just enough light coming from the light posts every hundred feet or so. I reached in my pocket for the cellphone but it was empty. Checking the rest of my pockets, I realized I had dropped it somewhere back in the hotel. Hopefully Quinton would realize we had made it out of the hotel by now and change his course. I still hadn't decided what to do once we reached the mausoleum.

I continued towards the cemetery, breaking several traffic laws on the way over. I was glad that I was familiar with where the cemetery was, since cell phone navigation wouldn't become commonplace for at least another three years. After a few minutes on the road unfollowed, I slowed down to avoid suspicion.

From the blank look on her face, it seemed Olivia was still processing everything. Even in that stressful situation, she handled herself well. If it wasn't for her, I'd still be stuck in the elevator, or maybe I would have had to knock out that valet.

I took my right hand off the wheel and touched her hand. She broke out of her daze and caught my eyes for a moment before I looked back to the road. Her grip tightened as she went back to thinking.

At our current rate, it would take us about twenty minutes to reach the cemetery. I opened the window a crack to let the fresh, warm air hit my face. I forgot about being stuck in a tug of war that I didn't belong in. My mind drifted over to Olivia's dreams of us being together. Me surviving the gunshot and living happily ever after with her. If that was even possible.

For the first time in years, I felt like maybe love was possible. Along with my past, I'd buried any notion of intimacy beyond the physical. After seeing Lijuan in such pain near the end, it blackened my heart. Olivia made me feel like I wanted to love again. Or at least try again. I looked over at her to see her looking back. She glanced away and stared out into the distance.

"You know," she said. "I didn't want to tell you this but..." she choked up, the smallest tear in her eye. "In my last dream..." I remained focused on the road and sat in silence as she found her words. "You died. I wasn't sure at first, but I remember it now." She watched me, expressionless. "That woman back there, she came for you. The old man tried to stop her, but it was too late."

I mustered up all the optimism I could. "We have another chance. Now is all that matters."

The car zoomed through the city, making good time. I monitored the mirrors, feeling relief each time I saw they were clear. The cemetery was less than two miles away now.

Olivia sat up and leaned against the headrest. "Another chance...I think I tried to fix it...I tried to warn you—"

I took a sharp turn when suddenly something rammed from behind, causing us to propel faster forward and then spin wildly. I gripped the wheel hard but couldn't fight against the force. While spinning in several 360 rotations, I caught glimpses of a black SUV now speeding behind us. Its lights were off, making it almost completely invisible if not for the moon's reflection.

I pulled hard on the clutch and shifted into another gear while hitting the brake, shocking the car out of the spin so the tread could grab onto the asphalt. It wobbled like I could lose control at any second but eventually righted itself. The SUV slammed again, this time from a much closer position. I kept control of the car, even as it shook and several of the emergency dash lights lit up. Olivia grabbed on the side of the door, trying to stay calm as best she could.

Sweat dripped down my face as the nervousness in me grew. In the distance, construction barrels and equipment lined the freeway. In my rearview mirror, the SUV sped up, readying to ram us for a third time. Just as it approached, I cut the wheel and veered into the left lane and decelerated. The SUV passed by a few feet now, giving me a chance to fight back. I turned hard to the right, pushing them further into the shoulder, putting them directly on a path into a construction barrier. It crashed hard into the concrete sending blocks of cement and steel into the air.

Olivia and I both exhaled a sigh of relief that was short-lived. With the SUV gone, we realized it had been blocking the view of the silver BMW I had become all too acquainted with.

In the near distance, I could make out the cemetery but the gates looked locked shut. A tall cement wall surrounded the perimeter. We'd have to enter on foot or hope the car wouldn't crumple into a piece of paper after ramming the gate.

Deciding not to risk certain death, I drove on now less than a block from the cemetery. Easily within walking distance. The BMW sped up, trying to take its place behind me.

"Hold on!" I screamed to Olivia.

The silver car raced straight towards us as I slammed hard on the brake. The BMW smashed into the back of our sports car destroying our bumper—and their own front cabin. My neck shot forward, launching my face into the airbag that exploded and wrapped around my face.

30

The harsh smell of smoke and burning filled the air as I reached around for Olivia. With my face still in the airbag blinding me, I found her hand and she squeezed it tight. My stupid plan worked and we both survived. I pulled my head back and fought the bag away to see her dazed, but okay.

I pushed my door open and stumbled out, holding my neck. Walking around the other side, I pried Olivia's door open and helped her out.

"You okay?"

She coughed from the smoke and nodded, but her eyes winced with pain. I'd imagined she had the same shooting pain coming from her neck. I looked back to the mess I caused and saw the silver car totaled—melted hot steel linked the cars together. The BMW compressed like an accordion when it hit our trunk, giving us enough buffer not to be smashed. If I had anyone in the backseat, they wouldn't have survived.

The cemetery was now less than a minute's walk. As

we hobbled closer, I saw Quinton on the other side hammering away at the giant padlock blocking our way.

"They tried to lock you out after I came in!" he said, over the loud banging of his crowbar smashing the steel.

We approached the gate while he continued working on the lock. He stopped and looked behind us.

"Great." He resumed slamming away at the padlock, now showing signs of warping from the abuse.

Behind us, another black SUV pulled up, bright lights beaming. Before it stopped, its doors blew open and three men in suits hopped out. With a loud crack, Quinton broke the padlock and started pulling off the chain. One of the suits pulled out a pistol and kneeled into a cover position while the others rushed forward.

"Go!" I said to Olivia as the men raced closer.

Quinton pushed at the gate but it soon locked in position creating a small opening. After ensuring Olivia made it through, I followed close behind. With half my body through, a powerful hand grabbed hold of my shirt and pulled. I latched onto the cemetery gate, wrapping my arms through the bars. The gate swung outward from the force of the man's hand.

I began to lose my grip on the bars, sliding off finger by finger. Terror ran through my body as I saw the other suit lining up his shot. Suddenly, the gate swayed inward. I glanced over and saw Olivia and Quinton pulling me closer. The suit was strong, but he was losing his hold against them. The other man ran to his side and tried to grab my arm, but with one last pull, the gate swung all the way into the cemetery. I let go and tumbled onto the soil inside as they slammed it back into place.

The suited men watched through the gate in confusion, as if I was now masked by some kind of shield.

"They can't even get in." Quinton caught his breath. "Orchid's grunts."

Quinton fixed his eyes on Olivia, who was pacing through the rows of headstones. "That's her?"

I nodded. He walked over and put his hand on her shoulder. She stopped and turned to face him before jolting back and taking a few steps away.

"Miss?" Quinton lowered his voice in a soft whisper. She stopped after putting a few feet between them.

"Everything that you've seen today, that you might see —this will change how you look at the world forever. We have rules against letting outsiders near the circle, but in situations such as these, your bond with Hagaki allows us to plead a case for it."

She squinted her eyes, listening with intensity.

"You are going to be given a choice. Walk away as if nothing happened. You will have no knowledge of tonight and you will return to your life. Or, you make a case to bind to the Council. You won't be a full member, but you will have protection and," he stopped and motioned for her to walk with him. I kept my distance and followed behind. "Our secrecy will remain intact. You won't be able to speak, write, or communicate about us. There have been very few cases involving the binding process being allowed, but it is not unheard of if your connection to a member is strong enough."

The puzzled expression remained painted across her face. "I need—to think about this," she trailed off.

Quinton turned back to me. "Hagaki, come."

I jogged up beside them. "We're safe now, aren't we?" I said, keeping my voice low.

"Yes. As long as we're here, they cannot take action against you. And once you have been scanned, you are protected."

"How are we all part of Tempus if there is so much infighting?"

"Do you know of a country without internal war? Disagreeing opinions?"

"Well, then how were those men able to fight Alycia?"

"They may fight if the reasons are just, but the wounds will be non-lethal, even if they used bullets. Even lost limbs. Everything is temporary. The only allowed uses of lethal force are when protecting the secrecy of the Council and to ensure the stability of the timeline."

"Until me."

"You are correct. Your expiration was unauthorized and Orchid broke protocol. I was not even authorized to approach you, hence my secrecy. I prefer a more direct approach, myself, although I wasn't planning to intercept you for weeks. The number you called set off alarms on all sides."

I looked over to Olivia who followed beside us. She resembled a lost child straggling down the pathway. I wondered if she was listening to our conversation or still deciding what she would do.

"There." Quinton pointed in the distance to a large stone mausoleum in the far corner of the cemetery. It was overgrown with vines although the lawn surrounding it was well maintained. Off appearances alone, it was easily one of the oldest structures in the cemetery. "They are waiting for us."

I stopped walking. "Who are *They*?" Quinton and Olivia stopped a few feet later. He turned to me with a stoic look on his face.

"There's no proper answer to that. Most have been around longer than I have."

"I'm tired of the secrecy, Quinton. I don't know what I've signed up for, I don't know who else I might have dragged into this, and I don't even know what's even expected of me once I'm *scanned*. All I know is that I'm tired of running."

"You're doing the right thing. It will all be clear soon."

"I'm only doing this because after today, I don't think I have much of a choice. I ran from Japan when my brother and mother were killed. I ran across the Chinese countryside when the Emperor was overthrown and I had no place to call my home. I ran from Detroit because I wanted to follow my dreams and I had no family left."

Quinton's eyes exploded open like supernovas. It was an eerie, almost supernatural sight. He cocked his head to the left and started rubbing his long white beard.

"What are you talking about?" he said, wavering with nervousness.

"Part of me just wants to fight. Fight until there's nothing left. But I've been fighting for more years than I can count."

Quinton moved closer and looked directly into my eyes.

"What are you speaking of? Your dossier said nothing

of you traveling in Asia. You were born in Poland, immigrated to the United States at the age of five—"

"Enough Quinton, you know my past. The note you gave me. It was full of Ancient Chinese text."

Quinton's forehead beaded with sweat. He shook his head in disbelief.

"No, no. Not from me."

He walked closer and pulled at my shirt, exposing my bar code. My initial instincts caused me to pull back. He stared down at the code, which now had a light green hue.

"No." He backed away with his eyes still fixed on my arm. "No, this can't be."

Olivia finally snapped out of her daze. "What's going on?"

"How could I have missed it! Your markings, they predate even mine. You've been a traveler for much longer than we imagined, Hagaki."

"What does that mean?"

"You don't remember me, correct?"

I nodded. "You seem so familiar, but no, I don't remember."

"From what I've gathered, you already know that as travelers, when our life eventually expires, we continue in the next."

"I remember my life in China. I remember nothing else until this life."

"Exactly!" He was getting visibly excited. "Some of us, a rare few, carry over with more lives than two. Just now, when you spoke of an emperor. I knew you had at least a third we had been unaware of!"

"A third?" His words made sense, but they still gave

me that spinning feeling like I had just stepped off a tilt-a-whirl.

"Well over a hundred years ago in England. I felt your presence as soon as you arrived. It's indescribable, but as you said, you feel you know me as well."

Images started flashing into my head, sending me off balance. I righted myself but my legs wobbled. Olivia ran over and braced me. I saw Quinton. Much younger, a different face. But it was him. He stood next to me in the streets of London. A key turned in my skull, unlocking deep buried secrets.

"Yesss." I slurred out. I closed my eyes but I could feel them dart around inside my head as if I was entering REM. Bits of hazy memories surfaced. Some kind of trade. A blacksmith? "I lived off an uneven cobblestone street."

Quinton nodded with a sly grin. "We always travel in pairs."

"What is happening!" Olivia screamed. "What did you do to him!"

"It's coming back to him now. He's remembering."

Olivia held me tight while I continued to seize. Suddenly, the images stopped as quickly as they had appeared. My mind was blank for a few seconds. Something inside me was trying to protect my brain from overloading.

The feeling came back in my legs and I stood up on my own without Olivia's help. A calm washed over me. Whatever just happened had made me stronger, smarter, more whole.

"Yes, that's it. You remember now?" Quinton said.

I looked into his eyes and now saw my brother. His identical intense blue eyes radiated back into mine with a newly realized warmth. I nodded, silently acknowledging him.

"We must hurry. We've kept them waiting long enough." Quinton commanded.

We resumed following him. "But if the message was not from you, then who?" I said.

"I am not sure. It's possible it was one of the others. I only told you about the most common groups within Tempus. Smaller splinter groups, or even rogues may have their own interests in you. We are all bound by the same protocols. Some move more freely without following their superior's wishes."

"Like aiding a long-lost brother?" I laughed.

"Yes," he chuckled, "exactly. But I do not believe it will thrill them if they figure out I let you escape. I needed to keep my cover."

The sound of thunder roared in the background as we stood in front of the mausoleum steps. I looked up, in awe of how much larger it appeared up close. The noise grew louder, now emanating from behind us as we climbed upward. I turned to see two motorcycles roll toward us, their engines settling into a dull roar as they stopped near the bottom of the stairs. Quinton whispered something to Olivia and she ran into the building.

The riders dismounted and approached from the darkness. Alycia appeared, standing next to a tall, well-dressed man. They stopped at the first step and looked up at us.

"We won't let you go through with this!" Alycia shouted, rage in her voice.

Quinton recoiled in disgust. "I can't believe I'm seeing you two together! So Lucian, this brings you out of your ivory tower?"

Lucian smirked with arrogance. "At this point, our interests have become mutual, old boy." He gestured to Alycia.

"We're on pure ground, Alycia. What do you plan to accomplish?" said Quinton.

"He hasn't been scanned, dear lad," Lucian said.

Quinton's eyes flashed with fire. "There is no battle on these grounds! The Council will strike you down if you even try to stop us!" Quinton turned to me. "Hagaki, go in. I will hold them off as long as I can."

I looked at Quinton and shook my head. "No. I told you, I'm tired of running. We do this together."

"We're so close, you can end this now!"

"And then what?" I said.

Alycia and Lucian stood at the steps, smiling at the conflict they caused. In my side view, I caught a bright flash of chrome as Lucian pulled a gun from his jacket and fired. As the bullet exploded from the chamber, Quinton leapt in front of me, catching it high in the chest.

Lucian's eyes followed Quinton down, giving me enough distraction to jump from the steps and attack. I grabbed his arm and twisted his wrist, loosening his grip. I reached over with my free hand, pulled the gun from him and aimed it back. Predicting another attack, I jumped away fast enough to dodge Alycia's attempt to grab me. Still stepping backwards, I pointed the gun back and forth between the two of them.

"This ends here, now," I said, looking into each of their eyes.

With the gun still aimed, I crouched next to Quinton. He coughed and grabbed his chest. To my surprise, I saw only a few specs of blood on his jacket.

"We can't kill each other," he laughed, which turned into another cough.

"Yeah, but I can kill them, can't I? I'm not scanned in yet," I smiled, looking back to them. They stood expressionless, backing away in separate directions.

With a heavy sigh, Quinton stood up and brushed off his jacket, more focused on the dirt than the blood. "If that's a choice you can live with."

"I've killed enough people," I smirked while dismantling the gun into four large pieces. Pocketing the spring for my own safe keeping, I threw the rest on the ground.

With one last look back at Alycia and Lucian, Quinton followed me into the mausoleum and closed the door behind us.

31

———

The door's heavy thud reverberated through the dark corridor, illuminated by the flickering candles placed on the walls. We walked rows of gravestones, the names of the dead etched into the stone seeming to whisper to us.

At the first fork in the hallway, Quinton stopped and turned to face me. "Follow me."

"Where is Olivia? We should look for her."

"Come, I'm sure she is safe with them now."

I took his guidance and followed as he led me through the winding dark passages. The further we went, the more worn the hallways looked. It became darker, with short bursts of moonlight pouring through skylights every hundred feet or so. Through the dim light, I noticed the dates on the graves became older as we drifted through the hallways. Some dated back to the 1800s.

With every step, the candles grew dimmer and farther apart. Soon, the area ahead of us was completely dark, no moonlight to guide us further. Quinton grabbed one of the last candles off the wall and we continued onward. After a minute of walking we reached a dead end.

"Here, hold this." He handed me the candle and started feeling along the wall. "Shine the light closer, here."

I moved the candle closer, the light flickering and casting shadows on the walls. Quinton ran his hands across the nameless gravestone, feeling until finding the date 1798 - 1821. His fingers squeezed the numbers and pushed them apart. They slid with a click and locked into place, revealing a small electronic window. With a wave of his hand, a bright red light shot out of the window, illuminating the barcode that was now visible on his wrist.

"Stand back," he said, extending his arm as if to protect me from moving.

We both took a few steps back, feeling the vibrations of the wall as it shook with a loud rumbling. The bottom three rows of headstones sank inward, revealing a small opening. Quinton crouched and motioned for me to follow. We ducked under the wall and continued down a spiraling staircase that looked like it belonged in Dracula's Castle. Once again, the only source of light came from my candle. The stairs seemed to go on forever, twisting deep beneath the cemetery. The air was thick with the scent of wet soil, becoming more overpowering with each step. I heard my breath echo off the walls as I drew in the cold, earthy air. I couldn't help but question how far we had gone.

We finally reached the end of the stairs leading us to a small wooden door barely grasping on to its hinges.

"This is it, brother. Your chance for this to end. And begin."

He held the door open and gestured for me to enter. I stepped into a large hallway that resembled Pharaoh's office, lit by fluorescent bulbs. It was a shock to see such a modern-looking area after walking through the old musty corridors and staircases. Now further in, we came upon a large set of double doors. We entered together, each opening a door for ourselves.

I crept in and saw a medium-sized amphitheater built to accommodate a few hundred. In the center stood a hooded figure in a dark blue robe. As we descended, I looked around at the others in the audience. Twenty at most, scattered in various small groups. Some dressed in the dark grey suits I had run into earlier. The contempt in their eyes was palpable as I passed.

In the far corner sat a couple dressed in the same skin-tight leather as Alycia. Their gaze remained locked forward at the center. Pharaoh sat amongst a few others, their whispers punctuating the silence of the room. The rest of the audience consisted of individuals keeping their distance from others. Most wore everyday clothing that matched the current trends. The rest were trapped in time, wearing clothing that dated a few decades earlier.

I reached the center and stood on the dark red carpet covering the floor. Olivia sat in the front row, her hands clasped in her lap. Next to her, a stranger. Bald, looking to be in his seventies with a tailored black suit that appeared flawless. Olivia looked into my eyes, then at Quinton, and then back towards the figure in the middle. Her eyes were empty, devoid of emotion. In my gut I felt the worry build. Whatever she decided was her choice, after all, but I selfishly hoped she opted to remember.

"Welcome," the robed figure said from the center. "We've been expecting you." The ethereal voice gave no hints of age, sex, or gendered expression.

"I apologize for our tardiness, One," Quinton said, followed by a bow. I thought it best to follow his lead and bowed as well.

"No need, Traveler Quinton. I am aware of the transgressions that have taken place within our sanctuary." Just minutes ago and they already knew. Impressive. "Those responsible will face their just punishment immediately after our session has concluded. Please be seated, Quinton."

Quinton bowed again and took a seat in the first row. The figure turned to me.

"Hagaki," the voice boomed through the amphitheater, sending chills down my spine. "Please step forward."

I stepped closer and came within several feet to face them. Even up close, it was difficult to see any detail.

"You have been charged with the most ultimate act of time violation ever recorded." They paused for a moment and looked around the audience.

Either I had misheard Quinton, which I didn't think was the case since I hung off his every word, or this had turned into my trial. Even in the cold underground chamber, a nervous wave of heat passed through me. I looked around the room to see all the faces staring back. My breath became labored and beads of sweat accumulated on my forehead.

"However, upon review, we have granted you leniency. You have done this unbeknownst to yourself and without malice or evil intention. While balance has been significantly disrupted, Tempus exists solely to restore it."

The fear disappeared. The invisible hands around my neck had let go, allowing me to breathe again.

"You have traveled quite far, Hagaki. We have sought you for centuries now since we last parted. While you may not remember your past with us, it will return, in time."

I looked at Quinton, nodding his head. The others sat motionless.

"Your presence here, of your own free will, signifies you have returned to reclaim your status within the Council. You must now choose your alignment."

The robed figure extended their hand to me, palm facing upward, letting me know the floor was mine. Muffled voices filled the room until I moved closer and cleared my throat. The noises died, leaving me to speak alone in the silence.

I looked into the faintly visible dark eyes. "I plead..." I closed my eyes and swallowed hard. A sudden, sharp pain exploded in my mind and the vision of a translucent white blossom disappeared as quickly as it came. I regained my composure as the pain faded. "I plead neutrality."

The crowd erupted with chatter. I saw Pharaoh throw his fist upward in outrage. The suits remained stationary.

"Order!" One shouted. "Very well, Hagaki. Step forth."

I walked until I was directly in front of One. They

raised a hand and placed it on my arm. A loud crash erupted from the top of the amphitheater as the entrance sprang open. With the doors almost off their hinges, Alycia entered first, followed by Lucian.

"Stop this at once!" Alycia screamed from the top of the stairs. Lucian bolted down the steps, speeding towards the center.

One appeared not to notice the interruption as they continued pressing their fingers to my skin, over the barcode. I felt a warm sensation pass over my body, lightly at first, then building up to an extreme heat. Even through the fire, there was no pain. I imagined my nerve endings dancing, shooting electrons in every direction with no order. The warmth disappeared and every part of my body felt like it had received the deepest massage.

Lucian reached the center but was pushed back by an invisible barrier that sent him tumbling. He shot a look at the other suited men in the audience, but they looked away, offering no assistance. Upon seeing this, Alycia turned back, only to have the large doors slam shut. She pried at them but it was useless. They were sealed.

One last jolt of lightning swam through my veins. My chest extended outward, overly exaggerating my posture.

Laughing in gravity's face, I rose off the ground for a short moment. The electricity faded and I fell onto the carpet.

From the ground, I could see One eyeing Lucian and Alycia. They extended a gloved hand in their direction.

"You dare disturb the sacred ceremonies," One shouted. "Your judgment is next."

With a flick of a wrist, they both stood straight and motionless. One turned their gaze to me.

"Welcome Hagaki, assigned as neutral. Due to your past and current relationships, I have assigned Quinton as your guide. You are invited to return here in two months' time. You are free to leave."

I stood without a pain in my body. My vision felt sharper, like I had swapped out expired contact lenses with a fresh pair. The cool air on my skin tingled in the barely noticeable breeze. The chamber had a new smell to it, dried honey and burning wax. Every sense had experienced an upgrade.

I walked over to Quinton and sat next to him. We watched as others in robes appeared and carried the motionless bodies of Alycia and Lucian to the center of the room.

One raised their hands and spoke for a final time. "We shall adjourn this meeting on the next full moon. Until then, these two will remain in our custody. Fare thee well."

One turned and walked up the opposite aisle we arrived from. The robed figures followed soon after. Some audience members stood to leave as others began talking amongst themselves. I looked for Olivia but saw that she had already left, with the bald man nowhere in sight.

"She's gone," I whispered after a deep sigh.

I sat in silence until a majority of the members left, leaving us alone with the frozen statues of our attackers.

Quinton finally broke the silence. "You don't know what she chose."

"Who was that man with her?"

"He's one of the Originals," he paused and turned to me, "like you."

"Originals?"

"One knew you, the old code on your arm, being able to shift back seven years. Yes, you're one of the eldest Tempus members, whether you remember or not."

"What does this mean?"

"It means whatever you want it to. In time you can choose to remember, or you can continue on your own way. As long as you uphold your membership and contribute when needed, the world is yours. And I'll be here to help your transition."

I let his words bounce around in my head until I pointed to the statues in front of us. "What happens to them now?"

"They face the first cross-sect tribunal we've ever had. I believe this will help to restore the balance, even if both parties use their respective member as a scapegoat. For the time being, it will bring them together for a common cause. Now that you're neutral, they have no reason to quarrel over you. Rather, let me correct myself. They can't do anything about it."

I nodded and sat back in the chair, enjoying the

silence. I exhaled deeply feeling complete relief. My lips began to curve into a smile, but inside I couldn't stop thinking of Olivia.

Quinton read the concerned look on my face. "Whatever choice she made was the right one. You need to want what's best for her."

He was right. I wanted to be selfish. I wanted her to be with me now that we were safe. I wondered what that man told her and where she went.

"Yeah, you're right." I stood up. "There's still a chance she decided to stay, isn't there?"

Quinton stood and we started up the stairs to the exit. "Anything is possible."

EPILOGUE

A week had gone by after the whole ordeal and I hadn't heard from Olivia. I had locked myself inside, trying to make sense of the past few days but my brain started to hurt.

A soft knock on my door roused me from the sofa. I peaked out into the hallway. Empty. Before I closed the door, I noticed a small leather-bound journal. Written inside, Olivia had recounted the days leading up to her disappearance, giving me a bit more insight into our interactions.

After wallowing over how things ended, I worked up the nerve to finally leave my new apartment, generously provided by Quinton.

I took a trip downtown to visit the record store AJ worked at. I had a good feeling he'd be there—from what I remembered in his biography, it would be just about a few months before he had his big break.

I only met him a few times before I had traveled back. He seemed pretty easy to work with from our limited time together and I always thought highly of him. Banking on the possibility of that time residue thing, I hoped he would remember me in some way. I walked into the small record store and saw him opening a box with a pocket knife. I pretended like I was looking for something and then approached him as he pulled CDs out of the box.

"Hey man," I said.

He turned around and smiled. He looked a lot more clean cut than I remembered.

"Hi there, looking for anything in particular?"

"Yeah, actually. Yours, I hear you're pretty good."

He grinned and shook his head, dropping the retail service act. "Naw, you're just playin' with me!"

"No, seriously. I heard your latest from a friend, you've got skills man." I lied, only about where I heard the music, of course.

"Wow, thanks!" His smile beamed from ear to ear. "I'll grab you a copy from my truck!"

He yelled something to the other employee and ran out the back door. In under a minute he was back with a copy of his CD, complete with a handwritten sharpie label.

"Thanks! I've been looking to get a copy. Are the rumors that you've been signed true?"

He laughed. "Stop messing with me!"

"Well, I heard Paradise Records treats you like shit, remember that." I winked and shook his hand, then walked out of the store.

I laced my shoes tight and started a jog around the downtown area until I took a break to appreciate the lack of chaos in my life. I found myself sitting on a bench for ten minutes, taking in the energy of the city around me. I closed my eyes, listening to the conversation of a vendor across the street, excited about a new product he was selling.

"Mind if I sit here, son?" I broke from my trance and looked up to see an older man smile at me, pointing at the bench.

"Oh, sure."

"Thanks."

He sat down next to me and smiled again, exaggerating the wrinkles of his dark brown skin. The warmth in his green eyes put me at ease, feeling my muscles relax as he settled in.

"I see you're taking a break from all that running." It sounded more like a question than a statement.

"Enjoying the breeze, it's beautiful out," I replied.

"It truly is. I don't get out much these days."

I felt a powerful energy radiating off the man. I looked to see him staring across the street, watching the pedestrians waiting for the light at the crosswalk. An overly impatient man darted across the intersection, just barely avoiding a car. The older man shook his head.

"Not everyone plays by the rules, huh?" I said with a chuckle.

We watched as the impatient man tripped on the curb and landed in front of us. Papers scattered from his broken briefcase, littering the street.

"Time finds a way to work itself out though, doesn't it?" he replied.

A bus screeched as it pulled up and opened its doors.

I looked over to see the bench empty with the man already walking away down the street. "Take care, Hagaki," he yelled, his back to me.

I debated following but I felt an even stronger pull to see where the bus would take me. I had no destination in mind and all the time in the world. I climbed up the stairs and walked over to the middle of the bus, passing several open seats until I stopped dead in my tracks. Olivia was sitting by herself, staring out the window. I walked closer and stood next to the seat.

"Hi there," I got her attention. "Is this seat taken?"

She gave a warm smile. "Hah, there are plenty of open seats...but sure."

"Thanks," I smiled back.

"You look familiar. Have we met before?"

Thank you for reading!

If you enjoyed this book, please consider leaving a review and sharing with a friend.

And keep a lookout for the continued adventures in the Tapestry of Time, coming in 2024.

For all the latest updates, visit

https://www.steventemplar.com/ and sign up for the newsletter!

ABOUT THE AUTHOR

Steven Templar began writing his first novel over a decade ago, until it was finally released in 2023.

Steven loves travel, nature, animals, and of course, great storytelling.